A Gradiant Into Shadows

Stuart Mascair

Copyright © 2024 by Stuart Mascair

All rights reserved.

No part of this publication may be reproduced, distributed, or transmitted in any form or by any means, including photocopying, recording, or other electronic or mechanical methods, without the prior written permission of the publisher, except as permitted by U.S. copyright law. Except by a reviewer who may quote brief passages in a review. For permission requests, contact StuartMascair@gmail.com

The story, all names, characters, and incidents portrayed in this production are fictitious. No identification with actual persons (living or deceased), places, buildings, and products is intended or should be inferred.

Book Cover and illustrations by Luisa Galstyan

1st edition 2024

To all my professors at the Institute of American Indian arts. For broadening my horizons and teaching me my craft.

A Gradiant Into Shadows

Stuart Mascair

A Gradient into Shadows

Ptolemy and the Tiger

Ptolemy indulged in his usual morning routine by sleeping in the flower box on the porch banister. His white fur with spots of cinnamon red did little to camouflage him among the purple lavender. Ptolemy didn't care, as it was the most delectable sleeping spot in the entire cul-de-sac. This was the best place for soaking up the sun's rays from mid-morning to late afternoon.

A single bee, drunk on lavender pollen, buzzed and hummed around the cat's ears and face. She knew it would be best to mind her own business, but she also knew that she had the juiciest piece of gossip in the neighborhood. Ptolemy's ears twitched to get rid of the buzzing around his face. Upon failing, he awoke, yawned, and surveyed the porch.

"How do you do, Mr. Ptolemy?" asked the bee as she buzzed toward a stalk of lavender.

"Who woke me?" chirped Ptolemy, looking around before spotting the buzzing bee.

"I am surprised you are napping considering the news," said the bee.

"What news would that be?" he asked, stretching his legs out, his long claws curling out of his paws.

"Oh, it's not my place to say such things," said the bee. Ptolemy stood up, stretching his back before licking his paw. The bee vibrated with anticipation. The gossip was heavier than the pollen clinging to her legs. Once she told the news, she would surely be lighter.

"Miss Bee, I did not bother you while you went about your business, you were the one who woke me up from mine. So, would you kindly tell me what is so important as to interrupt my wonderful nap?"

"Well, Mr. Ptolemy, it's just that…well, you see…how

should I put this?"

"In your time, Miss Bee," chirped Ptolemy, weighing the pros and cons of eating the tiny insect.

"Well, I heard from one of the other drones who smelled of the most luscious dandelion pollen that Tiger the cat had given you quite the thrashing about a week ago," said Miss Bee with a flurry of buzzing.

"Well, that is simply not true. Tiger has never put so much as a claw on me," said Ptolemy.

"It's nothing to feel ashamed about. We all know you went to the vet last week; we just didn't know why."

"I was taken to the vet against my will, for all the usual reasons," yowled Ptolemy. "Not because that two-bit tabby beat me in a fight."

"Well, it's your word against his, Mr. Ptolemy. I just felt you ought to know what Tiger is saying about you," said Miss Bee, gathering more lavender pollen with her back legs.

"You know, you bees wouldn't be such busy bodies if you didn't have those little thorns in your behinds," said Ptolemy before hopping out of the flower box and onto the porch.

"Where are you going Mr. Ptolemy?" asked the bee.

"To put the claws to Tiger for running his big mouth," chirped Ptolemy. The bee was fortunate to get such an early scoop on the latest gossip.

As for Ptolemy, he began to make the rounds through the neighborhood. There were several places where he could find Tiger. The most obvious was at his residence across the street. There was also the playground he liked to defecate in, and the catnip patch all the cats loved to gather around in the old widow's backyard. Tiger, like all cats, was both predictable and evasive. Ptolemy just had to search through each of Tiger's haunts, even if it took all day. This was a clear sign of his dedication to finding Tiger and correcting the wrongs done to Ptolemy's good name. As he crossed the street, Rasputin the crow flew down next to the cat.

"Ptolemy! Good buddy, old pal, any chance your old lady is going to toss any popcorn on the lawn today?" asked Rasputin, hopping along to keep pace with Ptolemy.

"My Cynthia doesn't have those barbaric grandchildren until the day after next. That's when she always comes back with half a bag full of the stuff," said Ptolemy.

"Then I will just have to live with the memory of that bag of chips I found earlier. The treasures the tall ones cast aside are truly astounding," said Rasputin.

"If you say so," said Ptolemy with feigned politeness.

"You're in a mood today, my good man. Are there ticks in your coat? Your old pal Rasputin could pluck them out, you have but to ask."

"I don't have ticks in my coat!" hissed Ptolemy. "Now flap off before I have you pounced."

"Such violence from such a close confidant; your whiskers must be in an uproar. Is it another rejection from the Lady Blue? Or perhaps you are still sore from the utter thrashing Tiger gave you last week?" said Rasputin.

"He did not beat me in a fight!" yowled Ptolemy before swiping at Rasputin. With his mighty wings, the crow flew himself out of reach of Ptolemy's extended claws, landing lightly with a bouncing hop.

"Apologies if I gave offense, my good man, my chum, my confidant. I did not invent the story, it's all the bees are talking about, and by extension the rest of the cult-de-sac. So, I do believe I have found the thorn in your paw."

"Well," said Ptolemy, sitting on the concrete and licking his coat briefly in an expert display of one of the core principles of cat etiquette: nonchalance. "Then it is my job to correct that absurd assumption. The bees care not for truth, only the intrigue of the idea. I am going to find Tiger and show everyone that he couldn't beat a kitten, let alone a true rogue such as myself."

"Aw, and I thought my day would be boring. I had not expected to find such a grand tale. A brave cat on a quest to clear his name, with his true friend and closest chum by his side to speak the truth on his behalf, to bear witness to his gallantry. I would be honored…" Ptolemy had already started walking off before Rasputin could finish. The crow bounced forward, following behind the cat.

"Hey, I wasn't done relating my role in your quest," said Rasputin.

"It seemed you were just warming up, and I don't have all day for you to monologue, and stop following me," replied

Ptolemy.

"My apologies, I should have realized you have the glower of a determined feline. It was foolish of me to dawdle on such an insignificant part of the story as myself," said Rasputin as the pair paced down the sidewalk.

"You're still following me."

"Pay me no mind, good pal, I am merely the witness to your deeds today," replied Rasputin. Ptolemy stopped. He had caught a scent in the air, the scent of Pickles the dog. Ptolemy's claws flexed in the sheaths of his paws. Pickles lived with Tiger, so it seemed reasonable that he might know what Tiger was doing. Ptolemy followed the sent to Tiger's house; the only barricade was a freshly painted fence.

Ptolemy hopped onto the rounded pillar that acted as a hinge for the gate. In the process, he got paint on his feet and tail. Pickles was asleep in the garden, his mouth covered in dandelion pollen. Pickles' coat was curly brown, and his floppy ears made him less intimidating than other dogs Ptolemy had seen in the neighborhood. This was a pampered pooch of the highest degree. Rasputin flew up on the fence, cocking his head to survey the yard.

"Oh well, no Tiger. Where else could he be?" asked Rasputin.

Ptolemy took a moment to lick his paw. The paint tasted metallic and rubbery. This was similar to when Cynthia's grandchildren painted his claws. He would have to find a birdbath to get the terrible taste out of his mouth.

"Don't know, but I think that dog is sure to know," said Ptolemy, smacking his mouth to get rid of the foul taste of paint. He hopped down onto the grass, his soft pads muffling his fall. The grass had been mowed recently, with large clumps of shredded blades clumped over the evenly cut lawn. The smell of cut plants was everywhere, almost overwhelming his acute nose. Thankfully, Pickles didn't have to be found by smell. Ptolemy crouched low, and with slow, precise movements, stalked his way forward. Every step was placed with great delicacy and intent. Rasputin watched Ptolemy as the cat slowly made his way across the lawn. Rasputin said nothing but could not stop himself from hopping and bobbing in place.

Pickle's legs twitched and wiggled as he chased rabbits

and squirrels in his dream. Ptolemy crouched down low as a precaution should Pickles awake. The dog stayed asleep, and once Ptolemy was convinced of the fact, he continued his stalk. Soon, Ptolemy was close enough to pounce on Pickles. He found proper footing with his back legs, his tail swaying back and forth with excitement.

He pounced.

Ptolemy pushed off the ground with his back legs, and the distance was closed. His claws sank into the sleeping dog. Pickles yowled in surprise, confusion, pain, and terror. He tried to escape the whirlwind of clawed swats to his head and back and only managed to back himself against the wet fence.

"Help! Help!" cried Pickles.

"Where is Tiger?" hissed Ptolemy with a paw raised to strike.

"What? Ptolemy, why are you scratching me? What did I ever do to you?" he yowled. Big splotches of paint clung to his coat.

"You know where Tiger is! Now tell me!" hissed Ptolemy.

"I don't know! I haven't seen him all morning," said Pickles. Ptolemy lunged at Pickles and sank his teeth into the dog's large ears. Pickles howled with anguish at the renewed attack.

"Lady Blue!" shouted Pickles. "He said he was going to find Lady Blue today; he said it last night."

"Is that the truth?" growled Ptolemy as he bit harder, eliciting another howl of distress.

"Yes, yes!" howled Pickles. The house's screen door flew open, and Tiger's human companion, Doreen, came out holding a broom.

"Ptolemy, you little bully," growled the human as she used the broom to separate Ptolemy and Pickles. "Go on, shew! Get! Get out of here!"

Ptolemy yowled as Doreen swept him toward the fence. Not wanting to be pushed around, Ptolemy ran to the fence, scrambling up the side, getting paint all over his belly.

"No, no, not the paint!" yelled Doreen with her hands on her head. "Stupid cat," she muttered as she tended to Pickles. "Poor guy, did that bully scratch you up? Let's see."

Ptolemy didn't wait around as he sauntered away, shaking his legs to get the clinging paint off his coat. Pickles' news was unwelcome. It was no secret that Lady Blue was the most eligible cat in the neighborhood. She lived in Gate Town, the walled community, and always ate the premium wet food. Much to the horror of her human companions, she was an exceptional hunter with a flair for catching birds. Lady Blue was gifted with a luxurious grey coat and eyes of blue ice. A fierce hunter in an opulent palace.

"An expert display of the rogue's stealth!" cawed Rasputin, "Pickles is not a small dog either. Twice your size by my eyes. But with the use of guile and ferocity, you put that hound in his place. A wonderful chapter in your saga. Did he give you directions to the boastful Tiger?"

"Are you still here!" hissed Ptolemy, turning to the crow.

"Oh my, your choler is still bubbling," said Rasputin, taking flight into the trees. "I do not take offense. I know how hunters can be. You are forgiven, my friend."

"I'm not your friend," chirped Ptolemy.

"Not true. Think of all the popcorn we dined on, think of all the adventures and scrapes we got into. If that isn't a clear sign of friendship, I don't know what is," said Rasputin, hopping on a lower branch.

"Ridiculous," muttered Ptolemy before crossing the street. Rasputin hopped on a higher branch to see the whole breadth of the street. Once on the other side, Ptolemy began to lick his fur in the driveway. Rasputin saw the car in the driveway, slowly backing out toward Ptolemy. Rasputin had many a feast from various critters that met the end under those monstrous locomotives. Ptolemy was in danger of getting run over. Rasputin extended his great wings and pushed himself up before dropping into a diving glide toward Ptolemy and the car.

"Car! Car! Car!" cawed Rasputin as he dove toward the distracted cat. Ptolemy, startled by the sudden noise, sprinted away into the bushes. The car jolted momentarily, and angry swearing could be heard from inside the vehicle. Ptolemy's heart thundered in his ears and chest as he watched the car continue to back into the street. Rasputin's cocked head poked itself into Ptolemy's hiding spot before uttering the greeting call.

"That was a close one, old chum. Lucky, I had such a commanding view of the street," said the crow.

"Yeah, lucky," said Ptolemy, leaving the bushes and continuing to the house's backyard.

"So, where to next, shall we go and meet Lady Blue?" asked Rasputin, bobbing behind Ptolemy.

"You think I would embarrass myself by presenting myself in front of her like this?" he said before squeezing himself between the iron bars that separated the backyard and the front.

"Then why are we here?"

"There is a convenient birdbath here," said Ptolemy upon entering the garden. Sure enough, a birdbath was in the back of the lush garden, overgrown with dandelions, thistles, and thick patches of grass. "A little bit of cleaning to get this nasty stuff off my coat."

"How very clever," said Rasputin, flying up to the basin's edge. Ptolemy followed him up with a light hop while carefully watching the edges of the stone basin. The two drank from the water that had been sitting there for days. It was filled with dirt and bugs, and the edges were covered in black and white bird feces. None of the elements were of any bother to the pair.

"Now let's get my coat cleaned," said Ptolemy as he began licking the paint and cleaning his mouth. So, engrossed with his cleaning, neither Ptolemy nor Rasputin saw the gang of pugs creeping out of the house.

"Cat! Cat! Cat!" barked the pugs as they charged out into the yard. Rasputin instinctively took flight; startled by the gang, Ptolemy slipped and fell into the birdbath. He was soaked and thrashed about to right himself. He tumbled onto the lawn before being surrounded by the pugs.

"Go away! Get out of here! This is our home!" yapped the pugs as they each charged the cat before retreating to a safe distance. As wet as possible, Ptolemy arched his back in his aggression.

"Back off, pugs!" hissed Ptolemy as the pugs kept barking at him.

"Get out of here! This is our house, and this is our lawn! Go, cat, get out of here!"

"Come here, you," yowled Ptolemy as he charged one of the pugs. The pug's flat face contorted in terror as he ran away from Ptolemy. The other pugs increased their barking and charged after the cat. Unable to catch the first pug, Ptolemy changed directions and charged another but was met with a similar result. Rasputin watched as the group chased itself around the yard and recalled a story a seagull once told him about sharks attacking a school of fish only to have the school evade the attack. Rasputin didn't know what a shark was or where there could be enough fish to be such a large school, but the notion effectively described what he saw.

"Begone feline invader, this is our home!" barked the pugs as they tripped over themselves to escape Ptolemy's claws.

"Rats and mice are less trouble to catch," hissed Ptolemy as he looked around at the barking pugs. "This is ridiculous, you are all ridiculous!"

"Hold strong, pugs!" shouted the leader. "We have him on the ropes!"

"That's it," said Ptolemy. "I'm wet, covered in this

goop, and I still have a real fight to get to. I'm leaving."

The pugs continually charged and barked at Ptolemy as he sauntered out of the backyard toward the iron gate. He hopped through the bars and back out into the street.

"The feline invader has fled!" shouted the leader. "We saved the house, now three cheers for we pugs! Hip, Hip, Hooray! Hip, Hip, Hooray! Hip, Hip, Hooray!" howled the group as Rasputin met up with Ptolemy on the sidewalk.

"What an absurd group of dogs," said Rasputin. "I think that part of the saga will need a little embellishing. Let's say they were much bigger, like big burly shepherd dogs, or lock-jawed bull biters."

"I think you should skip that part altogether," replied Ptolemy.

"Impossible, it has all the elements of dramatic tension. The hero takes a moment to collect himself and recoup before going in search of Lady Blue, only to be ambushed by a pack of ignorant ruffians. The story demands it."

"If you say so, though I think a confrontation with pugs isn't really worth praise."

"Nor do I, but what are you going to do now? You're soaked!" said Rasputin.

"Don't remind me," said Ptolemy before shaking his whole body, sending water droplets everywhere. "I figure I can save on daylight and head over to Gate Town, find a nice sunbeam to dry in. With any luck, Lady Blue will find me after I dry off."

"You mean find her?"

"In Gate Town, Lady Blue finds you," said Ptolemy as they made their way to the walled-off neighborhood.

It is not hard for a cat to get into a Gate Town. The walls are not too high, and plenty of trees hang over them. It seemed more difficult for humans to get in; why humans were so obsessed with walls, nobody quite knew. All Ptolemy had to do was find a decent tree to get in. The tree he did find was all covered in sticky sap that clung to his fur and paws. Ptolemy was in quite a state. The wet fur caused the dirt in his coat to turn to mud. Leaves clung to him, and with all the trips through various bushes, he had several burrs tangled in his coat as well. Ptolemy looked about and found a nice patch of sun on a porch.

"So, do we just wait here?" asked Rasputin as he hopped around the lounging cat.

"And what would I do otherwise?"

"Doesn't seem very proactive. Not really an exciting segment in the saga of revenge."

"That's where you are wrong," said Ptolemy, whipping his tail in delight. "Anticipation is everything: the slow suspenseful moments before the pounce, the languid gap between pets from your human friends. Good things come to those who wait."

Without a sound, Lady Blue pounced from her hiding place, her claws and teeth sinking into the back of Rasputin's neck. Ptolemy was on his feet, his back curled, and his tail aggressively puffed out.

"Ptolemy, I was wondering if you would show up today," said Lady Blue, holding Rasputin in place. "This is a wonderful gift you brought."

"He's not a gift. He's my friend, and you should put him down this instant," hissed Ptolemy.

"He's not? A pity, though I suppose I am not very fond

of crows," she said, taking her paws off Rasputin. The crow immediately took flight onto the banister.

"Goodness, I felt the great flock in the sky calling my name," said Rasputin, batting his wings. "Truly a dangerous cat. I am humbled in your presence."

"Crows. Always blabbering. Always talking," said Lady Blue, her ice-blue eyes staring straight into Ptolemy's soul. "They talk so much that it fills the minds of foolish cats with peculiar notions."

"Lady Blue," said Ptolemy, "I have a request."

"If it is a request for courtship, then you are quite foolish. If I didn't accept you before when your coat was pristine, then I most certainly won't now that you have crawled through the underbrush like an alley cat."

"It is not courtship I seek, not today," said Ptolemy. "Tiger has slandered my reputation, and I seek retribution for the slight against my name."

"Retribution," chirped Lady Blue in amusement. "Against Tiger? He came to me today when the night was broken by the dawn. He said he was now worthy of my attention. I suspect it was because of the duel you had with him last week. One that you lost, if I remember."

"I did not lose any fight with Tiger," hissed Ptolemy. "I am the victim of a vicious rumor. One I intend to clear up. I need to know where I can find Tiger."

"So, you can do what? Lose to him again? I have chased both of you off, and I know for certain that Tiger has sharper claws. You would be like a kitten to him."

"My claws are plenty sharp. Now tell me, where is Tiger?" hissed Ptolemy. Lady Blue lunged at Ptolemy, tackling him onto his back. She bit and scratched him with impunity, and he did everything he could to defend himself. Rasputin shifted and hopped on the banister. He wanted to help his friend, but he knew how sensitive the cat's ego was. No, he had to stay quiet and let it play out. Ptolemy yowled as Lady Blue sank her teeth into his neck. She bit harder whenever he wriggled or swatted at her with his claws.

"I yield!" yowled Ptolemy. Lady Blue held her bite, her tail swishing in satisfaction.

"Let this thrashing be a lesson on who you decided to

be rude to. I will brook no insult and will not tolerate any foolish or rude cats. Do you understand?"

"I do," chirped Ptolemy. Lady Blue let go of his neck and locked eyes with him. Her piercing blue eyes were daggers of pure ice that shook Ptolemy's resolve. He looked away. There would be no further challenge from him. Lady Blue chirped in satisfaction before stepping off Ptolemy, who immediately rolled away and began licking at his scratches.

"I sent Tiger away; he was not deserving of my attention, no matter what he thought. He said he would be waiting at the playground," said Lady Blue, licking her paws to clean her ears. "Now run along, Ptolemy, and if I see you around here again, I will not give polite conversation. Gate Town is mine. I can't have a fool of a cat walking around here. Other cats might think I'm getting soft."

With a feigned dignity that one only ever achieves from losing a fight, Ptolemy sauntered off. Rasputin took a moment to look over Lady Blue so he could do justice to her description. Lady Blue stared back with those blue eyes that frightened Rasputin to his very core. Then she licked her lips. The crow then thought it would be prudent to take his leave.

"Well, she really put the claws to you," said Rasputin, catching up with Ptolemy.

"It was nothing," lied Ptolemy. He had numerous scratches and bites all over his face and neck. He still couldn't help himself emitting a purr of satisfaction. "Lady Blue is warming up to me."

"Funny way of showing it."

"She is. The last time I went to Gate Town she immediately pounced on me and sent me home with a limp. This time, we had a brief conversation before she pounced on me, and as you can see, I am not limping."

"Well, it will be a wonderful chapter to your saga, I don't even need to embellish anything," said Rasputin.

"Well, maybe you could do a little embellishing for the sake of the story," said Ptolemy, climbing a tree to hop the fence.

"Yes," agreed Rasputin, "for the sake of the story. Even better, we have gotten our best lead on Tiger all day. The playground is not too far away."

"It isn't. Now would be the time to strike," said Ptolemy.

"Agreed, the final climactic battle on the playground."

It wasn't long before the two had made it to the playground. It was early evening, and all the children were playing on monkey bars, jungle gyms, slides, and a rickety merry-go-round, all while collecting gravel pebbles in their shoes, pockets, and sleeves. Ptolemy and Rasputin found Tiger being pet by three different children.

"There he is, the scoundrel," said Rasputin. "I am going to the trees to get an unobstructed view of the battle. You will have to tell me what you two say before exchanging claws."

"There won't be much said," said Ptolemy, watching his friend fly up to the nearest tree. Ptolemy looked at Tiger; his striped brown-black coat was well-kept and fluffy. He meowed in pleasure as the various children pet his back and scratched his head.

"Tiger!" yowled Ptolemy. "It is time for you to pay for the lies you have been spreading."

Tiger perked up and caught sight of Ptolemy. He rose

and arched his back in a stretch before moving toward Ptolemy.

"Ptolemy, well met," said the deep-voiced Tiger. "Word is that you have been picking fights all day. Am I next on your list of foes?" The two sat across from each other, following the ancient cat etiquette regarding duels.

"I have been looking for you all day. Now it's time to taste my claws," said Ptolemy. Many of the children began to gather to watch the two cats square off, emitting yowls and growls that sounded sinister and hoarse to their young ears.

"For what purpose? I have no quarrel with you. Is this about the so-called lies you mentioned?" asked Tiger.

"Yes, you have been spreading the word that we fought last week, and your triumph was so complete you sent me to the vet. I have come to prove that I have not lost a fight with you, nor will I ever."

"I have never said such a thing," said Tiger, his tail whipping back and forth. "What need do I have of dishonest words? My ego does not need bolstering." Upon hearing these words, Ptolemy began to think he might be telling the truth. The bees were notorious gossipers; maybe they had just heard the news about Ptolemy going to the vet, and the story twisted as it traveled from bee to bee.

"You think they are going to fight?" asked one of the children.

"I hope not," said another.

"I hope they do!" said a third.

"Maybe you are telling the truth. Even so," said Ptolemy, "I must save face. Even if both you and I know the truth, the neighborhood still believes the lie."

"I see," said Tiger. "Well, I do have a reason to fight you as well. I do have to teach you a lesson for what you did to my canine friend Pickles. He is a gentle soul, and I feel it is my duty to make amends."

"Then let us cross claws."

The two pounced on each other. Both Ptolemy and Tiger were solid and robust cats. They fought with ferocity and cunning as they slapped, clawed, bit, and kicked each other. At the height of their battle, two children pulled the two apart.

"No fighting," said the girl who held Tiger.

"You too," said the boy who held Ptolemy, who wriggled in his grasp.

"You got to grab him by the scruff of his neck, like how a mother cat does to the kitten. It makes them go limp," said the girl holding Tiger.

"Like this," said the boy, pinching Ptolemy's scruff. He immediately went limp, unable to move.

"Yeah, now you take him home to Mrs. Cynthia, I'll return Tiger to Mrs. Doreen," said the girl. The crowd of children collectively moaned before turning their attention back to play. Ptolemy was uncomfortable as the boy brought him back to his home in the cul-de-sac, but his firm grip held him in place.

"Wonderful fight, my good man!" cawed Rasputin overhead. "I will let the world know of your tale; we will talk tomorrow."

"Sure," yowled Ptolemy as the boy brought him to his home. The boy knocked and waited for the door to open. Cynthia opened the door to find Ptolemy and the boy.

"Hello, Mrs. Cynthia, Ptolemy picked a fight at the park with Tiger, so I brought him back here."

"Good heavens," said Cynthia, taking Ptolemy into her

arms. "Is he alright?" she said, looking him over.

"I think so. They weren't fighting long before we broke them up."

"Well, thank you, young man. I better take him to the vet just to be on the safe side."

A Gradient into Shadows

This story was first published in issue 6 of Old Pal Magazine in 2023

Letters from the Verdun Anomaly

These letters were written by Damien Neuville and were collected from the attic of his home in Bordeaux and have since been donated to the University of Paris. These letters have been translated by Sofie Brooks and offer an excellent view of the Verdun anomaly.

***

My dearest Lynette,

My heart swells with anticipation of the momentous events I am about to take part in. I have been given orders to take my place at the front. It is hard to explain the joy welling within my breast. France has called up a generation of its young men to take part in the most glorious event of our day. I am thankful I have been given the chance to prove my mettle against the Germans, for there is no greater foe in all the world. My only complaint is that we are being sent to a quiet sector of the front near the city of Verdun. While I understand the need to protect such a treasure, I find it difficult knowing that I will be a glorified gatekeeper when so many young men are spilling their blood to repel the invaders. However, I am honored that my efforts can be of service to France.

Many of my comrades in arms feel similarly. Every occupation is represented in our number, from lawyers, bakers, goldsmiths, farmers, architects, and dozens more, and oh Lynette, the Algerians! I have never seen so many in uniform. It gladdens my heart that so many from so far away are taking up the saber in defense of France. I feel out of place being a student of the finer arts of music and composition. I must continually remind myself that even though my occupation is not so physically demanding, my spirit will not be found wanting on the battlefield.

Even so, our commanders are very strict and are ever

vigilant for signs of sickly courage. Just yesterday I witnessed the execution of a would-be deserter. The man, Jean-Claude, was led away to the firing squad. But before the unfortunate wretch was executed, he was brought before the company for a demonstration in discipline. Our commander explained that he was not sentencing this man to death for dereliction of duty, but to safeguard the morals of France. Our commander explained that "this death will be in service to a higher cause, one that transcends the laws of man. A cause for the nation. His death would remind those whose souls are given to melancholy that we must remain steely of heart and mind. It will harden those hearts and remind them of their duty." I admit I was moved by the commander's eloquence. Jean-Claude was filled with such vigor that he walked to the firing squad with his head held high.

    He too was giving his life for France!

    I apologize if this letter has become distasteful or macabre, a side effect of living so long with hardened men, but I wish to impress upon you the realities of war. While perhaps I should shield you from such things, I gave my vows before God that I would be true and faithful to you. To hide the truth would be a sin against not only you but God!

That reminds me. Recently several German spies were captured wandering the fields of Verdun. They claimed they were archeologists on an excavation dig, but we saw right through their lies as they carried cameras of such sophistication that they could only be used for spying. They were in such outlandish garb as well. One had a shirt from a "band" called Ramstein, while another had a button of a mouse in red shorts. All seemed to favor denim trousers. They were taken away by the military police. The Kaiser will have to dress his agents in less conspicuous clothing if he wants to sneak into our lines.

Lynette, I miss you so. My heart aches when I think of you. I hope this war will be finished before you give birth to our child. I am thankful that if the worst were to happen, you at least have the family to look after. Even so, I will endeavor to give my everything so that we will be victorious, and we will be reunited. The sourest aspect of my adventure is that I do not get to hear your daily exercise at the piano. I am forced to relive your delicate handling of Debussy and Satie in my memory. War, in all its courage and bombast and grandeur, lacks the civilized sensibilities that can be found in your fingers once they touch the keys of a piano.

I miss you terribly,

Damien

16th of February 1916.

***

To my lovely Lynette,

I can scarcely believe my good fortune, as the past two weeks have been a trial. On the twenty-first of February, the Germans began their offensive to capture Verdun. It wasn't even dawn when they began their initial bombardment. There are no words that can accurately describe the hurricane of shellfire we endured. The sound alone would be unendurable by softer men. Not in all the world has anyone experienced what we have on this section of the front. A howling, roaring, thundering storm of shellfire. Absent were the pops and booms of individual guns as they fired off their munitions. I have trouble finding words for the sensation of all sounds being subsumed into the continuous thunderclap of explosions. The concussive waves were so great that they pressed on my skull like a vise. One can't even shout in such a cacophony as the words are drowned out by the explosion. I screamed in horror, but I couldn't even hear my voice amid the maelstrom. I only knew I was screaming because my throat became raw with the effort.

I haven't even spoken of the destructive power of these guns. The expert artillerymen of the enemy went about destroying every centimeter of the battlefield. Before my eyes, forests and hills were turned to mulch and powder. As though using a hose, the Germans showered shrapnel across Verdun and turned it into a brown smear of dirt. It was as if the whole landscape was picked up and shaken into new and alien shapes. The green grass has been replaced with churned-up dirt resembling mounds of brown sugar. What's left of the trees has been turned into splintered teeth. We dug into the earth like moles or rabbits, as to stay on the surface is to court death.

When the artillery finally ceased after who knows how long, we took our place on the battlements of the trench. Only one in five were capable of fighting; the rest were either blown to horrid pieces or buried alive in the collapsing trench. We waited for the incoming German attack. We were prepared to return the predawn bombardment with steel, and grit. To throw back the enemy with French blood and valor.

However, this was a German ploy to expose our positions. We were not greeted with the grey uniforms of men. Instead, we were met with another withering hurricane of German bombardment. I lived for two weeks fighting the enemy as they showered us with endless munitions. They stormed trenches with frightful flamethrowers that belched out fiery death. The foe was on the march, meeting more success in two weeks than they had in years of sustained warfare. They took fortresses, trenches, and killed so many young Frenchmen that my hand trembles as I write this. Even so, we threw back those brave and gallant warriors by the thousands. It is such a tragic thing to see those brave, stalwart Germans cut down.

Lynette, forgive the splotches of tears on this letter for I cannot hold them back any longer. I am sitting now at a café in Bar-le-Duc as part of the rotation program the army has. In another two weeks, I will be sent back into the trenches to do my part. While I don't feel myself a coward, I tremble at the thought of going back into that meat grinder. I will talk no more of the menagerie of grotesqueries I saw on that battlefield. It is not right for the fairer sex to be forced to imagine such horrid sights as a modern battlefield.

However, I must tell you of a most peculiar event that happened during my time in the trenches. It was either on the twenty-sixth or twenty-seventh of February when a man from no man's land stumbled into our trench in the middle of the night. The poor devil is lucky that he wasn't shot on sight. What was peculiar about him was not only his attire but his nationality. He was an American! He was dressed so outlandishly as he wore an oversized shirt depicting the tropics with a pair of shorts and a pair of brightly colored shoes. Around his belt was a pack that contained sundries, the most peculiar being a brightly colored currency called a euro. The man seemed to be dressed for the summer, not for early spring. One of our number who spoke a little English tried to ask what he was doing on a European battlefield. But he was so shocked by his encounter in no man's land that he only babbled. So, we sent him to the commander to get some answers out of that poor devil.

But Lynette, my trials on the front have proven that I am no coward. I have my strength, and you can be proud that I have endured the sights and horrors I have related to you in this letter. I am thrilled to know that Verdun is the site of a major German offensive. I will be contributing directly to the defense of France. I know for certain we can turn the tide here and throw the foe back to Berlin. For even if the earth and trees are laid low by German ferocity, you can be sure that French men will stand.

With all my love,
Damien
7th of March 1916

***

My joy, my Lynette,

I am to be rotated back into Verdun. Despite what my previous letters have mentioned I am filled with utter horror at being sent back into that maw that devours men and material like some diabolic beast. Even from the safe distance of Bar-le-Duc, I can hear the thundering of the cannonade as French guns seek to match the frightful outpour of German artillery. Men have been replaced with machines in this war. Fear rises in my chest when I think about going back to Verdun. I dare not refuse as just yesterday a man was shot for doing so. He was screaming how he would never go back, that he couldn't. I wish to call him a coward, but I know the words he shouted matched the words in the quiet of my skull. Lynette, to say that I am frightened does not do justice to the paralytic fear I feel at every waking moment. When I dream, I dream of the roaring guns and mutilated decaying bodies. The smell, Lynette. Remember that mouse you found dead in our cabinet last year? Remember how its rotting carcass sickened you so that you had to lay down to calm your nerves? That smell chokes Verdun. It sticks to your clothes, your hair and skin. God help me I shouldn't expose you to such horrors, but I need to voice these anxious thoughts. I hope you will forgive me. Despite my fear, I will not forsake my duty to France.

  Aside from my trepidations, there have been other peculiar sights in the area. There are strange planes that fly higher than any known winged craft or dirigible. A decent spyglass or binoculars show that these aircraft are not flown by pilots. There has been no consensus about where they come from or who they belong to. Our only clue is the U.N. stenciled on the side of these aircraft with an occasional symbol of the planet Earth as seen from above wreathed in laurels.

There have been other strange reports from the front, including strangers of all nationalities waking up in no man's land or the trenches, utterly bewildered as to how they arrived. Very similar to the American in the tropical shirt. But also, women and sometimes children! All dressed in strange ways. While some clothing is so bewildering it is difficult to describe, other clothing from these strangers is anachronistic. Some outfits go so far back as Napoleon's time.

Lynette, you may feel these strange occurrences may be what is important, but it is just part of the milieu of Verdun. A place that bewilders and horrifies in equal measure, a place where every day the world shifts and changes from the previous day's bombardment. There is no ground or terrain that remains the same. Even solid hills are warped or disfigured with craters, which in turn, are warped with more craters. The only precedent kept is the noise and the violence. Everything else is subject to change and uncertainty.

    My love, I hope you remain well and that my letters do not cause too much undue stress to you or our child. You must be the anchor for our family. Modern battles can range from weeks to months at a time, and my survival is uncertain. I pray to God that I will be one of the lucky ones to return home, for tomorrow I follow the sacred road back to Verdun where I will join my comrades against the foe. I love you with all my heart.

    Damien

    13th of March 1916

***

My Darling, Lynette

    The front is still terrible and atrocious, and the oddities continue to amass. The culprit appears to be that the laws of time and space have been torn asunder by the violence at Verdun. Today, a full legion of Roman soldiers marched into the middle of no man's land out of nowhere. Their formation was disordered as they fell within shell holes containing the putrid mess of rain, decaying flesh, and noxious gas. Their shouts could only be vaguely heard over the rancor of the battle. I commend the valiance of these men as they raised a wall of shields that were no match for either bullet or bombardment. These men who conquered all of Gaul in the Classical era were now being tangled up in barbed wire and shot to pieces. They raised their eagles high and tried to remake their formations, but they were turned to pulp and splinters. A grim reality, Lynette, but one I am accustomed to after so many endless days of ceaseless fighting.

 That was only one of many temporal accidents that have happened here. All the while those strange unpiloted airplanes fly overhead. With neither French nor German aircraft able to reach them.

 There was one instance of a plane dropping leaflets on the trenches. I managed to grab one and have enclosed it in this letter to you. The owner of these planes has a frightening knowledge of our predicament. However, we are to make no move to comply with the proposed cease-fire. The commanders were clear that the honor of France was at stake and that we should not jeopardize our position in case this is a German ploy. We are to hold our ground and continue our battle.

In your last letter, you mentioned that your brother was killed in the fighting north of here. Armond was a stout and kindly young man and I grieve for his loss. I'm thankful that you are with family to share these unhappy days. I wish I could be by your side instead of among this madness, but such is the nature of our time and the nature of war that seeks to keep our love apart. I am thankful that these letters see you well, and that one day we will be reunited.

Damien
19th of March 1916

***

Below is the pamphlet clipped to the March 19th letter with both French and German translations.

***

Eight Hundred Thousand Dead!

Soldiers of Verdun End the Madness End the Bloodshed!

Soldiers of the French and German armies, we the people of the 21st century beseech you to end the bloodshed at Verdun. Time and space are collapsing on this battlefield, and it is of great importance that you stop fighting so we may find a solution to this anomaly. We know that at this point in the war, Verdun is the most violent encounter to date. There are still two more years of violence ahead. Already the timelines have been contaminated, warping history and society! We have a solution that could fix the tear! But the violence around Verdun is too great to do any experimentation. Only you, the soldiers on the ground, can end the bloodshed that has taken so many lives and torn a hole in time. You must end the fighting for the good of the future. The modern governments of France and Germany are close friends and allies. Reconciliation is possible, friendship and unity are possible, end the senseless loss of life for minuscule gains. End the great tragedy that will only bring about an era of violence and bloodshed. We are doing everything we can to fix the anomaly. Now you too must do your part in the mending of our collective reality.

United Nations, signed August 12th, 2026

***

Dearest Lynette,

    I have been shot. Today a bullet grazed the side of my

neck. The injury is thankfully light, but it stings every time I move my head. The shot itself was not so severe to remove me from active duty. A part of me wishes that it hit me somewhere more severe that I would have an excuse to leave this God-forsaken hell. I know such thinking is useless as the march to leave Verdun is as costly and dangerous as the battle itself. The route between the sacred road and the battle lines is a quagmire of sucking, cloying, polluted mud that drags men down into its depths. We must follow a thin trail of wooden beams, and God in heaven help the man who falls into a shell crater. As the sides are too steep to traverse and the continuous bombardment makes rescue too costly an undertaking. So, we abandon men to their fate in those holes. I have seen others, half-submerged in the mud, having screamed themselves into an exhausted stupor. Most are men and sometimes women misplaced from their time, and as I said, there is little we can do besides offering a careful shot to the head to end their suffering. Lynette, I know my words may sound callous and cruel, not befitting a gentleman, but I can assure you it is a mercy for these poor exposed persons.

If not the mud, then there is the bombardment, if not the bombardment, there is the gas. My God the gas! It pollutes and clings to whatever it touches. It poisons the air and burns flesh. It mixes with the pools of fetid water filled with noxious corpses that bloat and disintegrate over many weeks.

It is a sign of our modern way of being when nothing can be counted on, not the earth that is remade on the whims of flying shells, or the poisoned air. Even time has been unmade, as it drops all manner of mysteries upon us. Only we endure in this man-made atrocity.

[Section indecipherable from splotches of mud]

—keep returning to the people of the future. Surely, they must have sophisticated artillery or advanced rifles that would turn the tide in this struggle. Why aren't these men from the future assisting anyone in the hasty conclusion of this conflict? Both German and French are a pair of punch-drunk fighters. Surely the introduction of fresh troops on either side of the conflict would bring about a speedy conclusion. When I mentioned this thought to another comrade, he laughed. He explained to me that these future nations probably want nothing to do with our conflict. If the pamphlets they keep dropping are to be believed, over eight to nine million will die by war's end. If this is true, then the future nations' refusal to take part in the fighting is understandable. But what keeps us fighting for such minimal gains with such astounding losses? I don't know the answers to this question. All I know is that we endure where we should not, and if some of the veterans are to be believed we may remain here for months at a time.

    I haven't even endured a full month on the front lines of Verdun, and I feel like I have been irrevocably altered by the experience. I doubt any of my future musical compositions will contain any drums. I think I have had my fill of bombast and explosive chords. I would not wish to hear anything louder than a flute or piano. All I ever hear is the sound of rifles, machine guns, and the ever-present artillery, mixed with the shouts of action and the whimpers of dying men. In truth, I only pray to see you again and hearing your dexterous hands on the piano. I think of the life that grows within you and I hold in my heart a promise of the future. Even if that future is falling into our present.

Damien

19th of March 1916

***

Lynette,

The nations of the future have a plan they wish to implement. The usual pamphlets were not forthcoming with specifics, but it has something to do with the delay of ti—

[Section indecipherable from splotch of mud]

Apparently, the numberless shells fired by both sides occasionally leave duds that will last over a hundred years and are still dangerous to the people of the future. I can't imagine this blighted land looking anything other than a vision of hell. I think it is a testament to the enduring nature of the human spirit and the fortitude of God's design that the land can one day blossom with green grass and vibrant flowers.

Our commanders are willing to participate in the future nations' plan on the condition that it does not jeopardize our position in the theater; whether our German counterparts are willing to participate is another story entirely. In truth, I do not have high hopes for this plan. Any sense of order or strategy dissolves into butchery. There is a futility in tactics in the face of such overwhelming brutish force. We can only pray to God that our actions are successful. So, we can protect the people of the future and the past from this horrendous battlefield. If only we could protect ourselves from this calamity. Lynette, I have seen so many of my countrymen perish in this battle. There are scarcely ten faces in a hundred that I recognize. Many having been killed and replaced with wide-eyed strangers. When I look upon the replacements it's like I am seeing myself from a month and a half ago. To my horror, I no longer recognize my features in the mirror. I find myself deconstructing my face and trying to gauge the person within. Who is this Damien Neuville, is he this dirty man in a uniform? Am I that dirty man with those cold sunken eyes? Never have I pondered these sorts of questions. However, at Verdun, they come easily.

    You see, time is not working correctly anymore. Sometimes I will be doing my duties and with a blink of an eye, I am transported to some other more serene land. One filled with grass and trees. A place with monuments to this battle I had fought in. I walk around these places in a daze. Maybe, I have survived this horror and grown old. That I can finally rest and relax and breathe freely. Then with the crack of a rifle or the shout of a coming gas attack, I fall back into this blighted hell. This seems to be happening to a lot of us, and it is driving men mad. Even without the sundering of time men were losing their nerve from the beginning.

I do not think you should worry too much as I do not think myself mad, but I must ask what is considered sane in a mad world. I am straying from the point. My pen follows my wondering mind when I should be telling you that I am safe and continue to be so. I am safe, and I will be rotated out within four days. For two blessed weeks of relative quiet, and the civilization of Bar-le-Duc. I will write to you then.

Damien
26th of March 1916

***

Another pamphlet was found clipped to the letter, this having to do with an operation called the "Nails of God." Translated from French and German.

***

Activate the Nails of God!

Soldiers of Verdun we have a plan to heal the tear in time. We have created sophisticated devices that use quantum mechanics to repair the damage in the temporal fabric. We will send them through the tear, and it is your duty to place them in specific places around the battlefield. They have been designed to interface with the technology of 1916. The idea is simple. The devices will be used and buried on the battlefield so that they may travel to the future in real-time. Once they are excavated, they will be activated to create a quantum entanglement to close the tear that is causing so much havoc with time. Your job is of great importance to the plan, as the violence on the battlefield may disrupt or destroy the devices. Both your respective nations and the nations of the future need you to give it your all!

United Nations, August 24th, 2028

***

Lynette,

I suffered a heartbreak today. I was cleaning my injury when a watchman shouted. I was at the ready, pointing my rifle toward the German line expecting a saboteur or possibly a line of grey-clad soldiers marching toward our trench. Instead, I saw a deer, a full antlered buck so regal and majestic in its demeanor that I could not help but yelp in awe from its magnificence. It had a noble bearing, and a clean coat indicative of a leisurely forest life. Its strength was obvious, and it elicited a cheer of delight amongst the weather-beaten men of our company. A similar cry could be heard from the German lines.

The tragedy was that this brave and noble animal was caught out in no man's land amidst the barbed wire, the shelling, and the pools of toxic water. The buck must have fallen through time as the wildlife had all fled from the horrors we unleashed onto this land. The animal with grace and poise hopped over tangles of barbed wire meant to trap the least agile soldier, whilst darting with ease around the pits of polluted filth. A roar of exaltation began to rise amongst us as we cheered on the animal to make its escape from that wretched land. The German cheers and encouragements met ours and the whole battlefield joined for this noble buck. A frenzied euphoria descended on us as we whooped and hollered, we clattered our helmets with ladles and stamped our feet with joy. For me, all the sound of the world vanished, and I could hear the delicate notes of Debussy's Clair de Lune play in my mind as I watched that noble animal make its way to safety. I could not stop the tears from tracing rivers on the dirt of my face, but I was not the only one stirred to such emotion. For the first time in a month, I have felt true joy. It was an affirmation of the human spirit and the enduring beauty of God.

Then a stray shell blew that noble animal to pieces.

The collective lament could be heard from the hearts of hundreds across this wasteland. Some of us swore, others punched the dirt walls of the trench with fury. Some of us, those whose hearts were protected with some strange indefatigable fortitude shook their heads in remorse and carried on with their duties. Lynette, upon seeing the sight of the murdered buck, my legs turned to jelly. I collapsed against the walls of the trench. It took hours before I could summon the strength to pull out my pen and write this letter.

I also wanted to let you know that I have been assigned to plant one of these temporal nails in no man's land. Thankfully, both French and German forces have agreed to a ceasefire so that we may safely seed this battlefield with the devices. One more evening of hard work and I will be safe again in Bar-le-Duc. I will also qualify for some leave time so that I may visit you once again. Indeed, this news has invigorated me into action, and I will do my utmost so that I can hasten our reunion. You may say I still have to wait a day. But the passage of time has little meaning for me anymore. It is only our meeting again that fills me with joy.

Till we meet again.

Damien

31st of March 1916.

***

Damien Neuville never returned home and was listed as missing in action on his March 31st mission. Neuville was later found wandering the fields of Verdun on December 9th, 1973, having fallen through time. He spent Christmas with his child for the first time, as well as his grandchildren. The photo below shows both Damien and the elderly Lynette playing the piano together.

A Gradient into Shadows

Jolen

Mary Lee took a fistful of red earth and threw it on her husband's descending casket. The mahogany box lined with white silk sank into the open maw of the earth, devouring her husband forever. The pain that Robert no longer felt only seemed to tighten in her chest. She wanted to throw that pain in the hole with him. The pain Jolene had given her. Tears would not come, even as the rest of the congregation wept and bawled like children.

So young, they said. Too young to be a widow, they said. I know you must feel horrible, they said. She pitied them. She was exhausted by them.

Mary Lee had already given her eulogy and felt something akin to relief that it was over and that she could return to feeling numb. She heard that one was supposed to live in grief, confront it, and feel normal about having it. That's what the internet said, at least. But Mary Lee didn't know if she was supposed to be crying like they did in a soap opera. All she knew was she moved like a robot, or a Mary Lee shaped dummy filled with sand. Some dim utterance brought her back to reality.

What was that? She asked, suddenly realizing who she was standing with.

I asked if you wanted to get a beer, said Sam, her brother-in-law. She looked him up and down at his turquoise necklace, black boots, black cattleman's hat, and expensive jacket over a black button-up shirt.

Sure, she said, taking his proffered arm as they walked across the brown cemetery grass.

Any bar will do, she said.

Yes, ma'am, he replied as he led her to his truck. She could feel the blocky silhouette of a pistol beneath his jacket.

That reminds me, she said as he opened the door, allowing her to step into the smoky cabin of the truck. Robert said you get his guns.

Even the Luger?

The Luger, both shotguns, the Springfield, Enfield, M1 Garand, all of them. They all go to you. Robert was very clear that they go to you and not his cousin Roger.

Sound decision, said Sam as he entered the driver's seat. Roger is a complete jackass.

Are you gonna sell them?

Don't know yet. Might get a fancy case to show them off or might just put them in my safe and forget about them. Mind if I smoke?

It's your truck.

They pulled out of the cemetery and onto the highway. They said nothing as they traveled down the long Texan road past the uniform trees and the numerous exits. Sam would occasionally flick ash out the window while blowing a puff of smoke out the side of his mouth.

I should quit these damn things. Now's the best time,

I guess, he said, crushing the butt of the cigarette in the overflowing ashtray as they turned onto the exit into town.

I guess so.

Maybe after this whole thing blows over.

Sure.

They drove into the parking lot of Gunther's Bar and Grill. They found a parking space, and soon, the pair found themselves in a booth near the bar.

Good afternoon. My name is Louisa, and I'll be your server for today. Can I get you started with anything? Asked the waitress.

Yeah, can we get a pitcher of beer? asked Sam.

I'm afraid you have to order food with that.

Well, let's see, does an appetizer work?

Sure does.

Well, get us some wings.

That comes with your choice of sauce. We have honey BBQ, sweet mustard, Gunther's secret sauce, wasabi Asian fusion, or plain.

Why don't you surprise us, Louisa?

Sure thing. Is there anything else I can get you?

No, thank you, said Mary Lee

Is everything alright? You two look like a pair of cats caught in a storm.

She just buried her husband.

Oh gosh, said Louisa, putting her hand on Mary Lee's shoulder. You hang in there, darling. Well, I'll leave you two to your grieving. I'll have that pitcher right out for you.

Thank you, ma'am, said Sam. When the beer arrived, they toasted.

To Robert, said Sam, raising his glass.

To Robert, she said, clinking the heel of her glass to his. They drank, he with a sip, she with a gulp.

You carrying a firearm nowadays? she asked.

Yes, ma'am, ever since those good old boys decided to beat me stupidly and send me to the ER last September. As soon as I was out of the hospital, I applied for a concealed carry permit. I don't intend to take a beating like that ever again.

I remember visiting you in the hospital, she said, sipping her beer. I usually had to drag Robert to the hospital for his checkups, but when he got the call, we were on the road before the motor had a chance to warm up. I didn't have a chance to say this then, but now is as good a time as any. I'm sorry.

For what? he asked

At the time, I thought you got what you deserved for your preferences in companionship. I thought a good thrashing would give you a wake-up call. That may be, you would find yourself a pretty nurse you could fall in love with and have some children. Get your life together. I don't know, but as soon as I saw what they did to you, I was heartbroken. Those tubes coming out of your mouth and nose, all that tape and stitches, I knew I was in the wrong. Nobody deserves what they done to you. I know you're a good man. I just hate that it took a risk to your life to see that.

Never thought I would ever hear you say such a thing, he said. I know that we've never been close. Hell, I know you were only being cordial with me all these years because of Robert.

Here are your wings, said Louisa, putting the red plastic basket of yellow-gold wings between them. I thought you would like the sweet mustard. It's my favorite. Can I get you anything else?

That will be fine. We might be here a while, so if you see the pitcher get low, could you top it off for us? said Sam.

Sure thing, darling.

Where was I? asked Sam.

How I'm a rotten bitch.

I have heard more unkind things from blood relatives than ever from you.

Still, I wasn't fair to you. I just wanted to apologize. You're family, after all.

Well, it would do me no good not to accept the apology of a recent widow, so I say we're square.

Mary Lee sipped her drink and decided to finish the glass.

I need to go to the lady's room.

Well, I'll be here, said Sam as she made her way to the lady's room.

Mary Lee leaned against the sink and took several deep breaths. But she could not keep the makeup-dyed tears from dripping into the sink. She wanted the tears to stop and contorted her face to dam up the welling of emotions that came up from her throat and out her eyes. The floodgates were open, and Mary Lee began to cry. It was loud, messy, undignified. A part of her thought it odd that a being called a widow would have had this kind of effect on her. Droplets of blackened tears continued falling, and Mary Lee could only hold onto the sink. The door briefly opened as another customer stepped in, saw the scene, and immediately left.

Darling? Are you alright in there? asked Louisa after a minute.

I'm fine, said Mary Lee, turning away from the waitress.

You don't sound fine. Here, I have some tissues in my pocket. Much better than those coarse paper towels, said Louisa, pulling the plastic-wrapped pouch of tissue from her apron.

Thank you, said Mary Lee, dabbing her eyes.

You know, I felt the same way when my daddy died about four years ago. He had a heart attack, took me a full ten minutes to get over the shock before I could call 911. They might have been able to save him, but a truck T-boned the ambulance. By the time they sent over the second one, it was too late. I felt guilty for a long time. If I had just called the hospital right away, he might have lived. It took me a long time to realize it wasn't my fault. These things just play out the way the lord Jesus thinks is best. Ain't no rhyme or reason for it. I can't tell you it will get easier, but I can say that ache won't hurt so bad.

 That's what they tell me, said Mary Lee.

 Take as much time as you need, darling. Don't fret about any of the other customers.

 I'll be fine. I gotta get back to my brother-in-law.

 Well, if you need anything, let me know, said Louisa.

 Wait a moment.

 Yeah, darling?

 Did you see her? When your daddy had that heart attack.

 See who?

 Never mind, it's not important.

 Well, give me a holler if you need anything, she said,

returning to the dining room. Mary Lee took several deep breaths before wiping up the running makeup and returning to the booth with Sam.

You doing alright? asked Sam.

I've been better, said Mary Lee, grabbing one of the yellow wings.

Robert's wings were better, said Sam, refilling his glass.

I have the recipe if you want it. He kept all his barbecue recipes in this little brown leather book. Had it been commissioned by a real bookbinder.

That's alright. I was never the cook between the two of us. I wouldn't know a skillet from a cake pan.

The doctors say the barbecue was what probably gave him stomach cancer. All that red meat and carcinogenic smoke or some such.

All those years working in that barbecue pit probably didn't help him much either.

Ain't that the truth.

So, what are your plans? Or is it still too early to be thinking about that?

Well, the house is paid for, no sense in selling it; I guess a lot of his stuff that he won't be using would be better off going to charity. I don't know, I'm not ready to think about that. I do know I'm going to get rid of that damn medical bed he spent so much time in. It's too filthy to give to charity. Hell, I might just burn it.

In this weather? Better not. I'll tell ya what: I have a friend who works at the dump. They got this big crusher they use for cars. I can convince him to crush that bed into a little cube.

That will work. She then sighed, wiping her fingers off with a paper napkin. You know, there was another woman right near the end.

Another woman? I find it hard to believe, considering his condition.

It's true. I found out about her when we still shared a bed. Before he moved to that godawful medical monstrosity. It was late one night in May, I think. He never was a restful sleeper, and cancer didn't help. He said the room was spinning and that he was falling into himself even though he was perfectly still.

That sounds awful.

It was worse with the stomach pain, and he was rail thin. God, he was the very picture of misery. Anyway, it was one of those sleepless nights when he called out her name. Jolene.

Anyone you know?

Nope, I went to his place of work to see if Jolene worked there. But no dice. I went through his old yearbooks, thinking it was a high school crush, but I found nothing. If it was a one-time thing, I would have let it go. But it wasn't. He started calling out her name a lot more in those late nights. One time, when I got out of the shower, I found her name written on the mirror, revealed by the steam. It was then that I confronted him about her.

I'm not sure I want to hear this.

I can stop, replied Mary Lee, as he topped off her glass of beer.

I don't know. I always had this picture of Robert as the perfect child in our family. He had better grades and didn't get in any trouble with school or the law. It's like seeing a chip on your favorite mug for the first time. I can't forget it. I can't ignore it. I want to know.

Well, alright then, she said, sipping her drink. I tried to hold back the anger for his sake, considering all the pain he was in, but it all came out one night when he was well enough to eat dinner. I asked him who the hell is Jolene. He denied ever knowing her. He didn't panic like he was caught red-handed. There weren't none of that. He seemed more…what's the word?

Perplexed?

Yeah, he said he didn't know any Jolene and had only eyes for me. Then he tried to prove it. Only he couldn't, not in the marital way, at least. Poor man. That may have been one of his better days, but he was in such bad shape.

I remember him near the end, said Sam. It's hard to believe he was once two hundred and thirty pounds.

He weighed one-forty when he died. Anyway, I figured the whole Jolene thing was some sort of bad dream. I could say I tried to put her out of my mind. But she was like a sore on the side of your mouth that you keep biting. It was about a month later when he took a turn for the worst. Had to practically live at that damn hospital. You saw him. He could hardly move. He was on the way out. I spent more time at that hospital than I did in my own home. I slept in those stupid chairs. I watched daytime television when Robert was knocked out from that cocktail of drugs.

    Got you a fresh pitcher, said Louisa, taking the empty pitcher and basket of chicken bones. Do you two need anything else to eat?

    Basket of mozzarella sticks, please, said Mary Lee.

    You got it, smiled Louisa, returning to the bar.

    Sweet girl, said Sam.

    Nice enough, she said, topping off her glass.

    Don't you think you're knocking those back pretty quick? asked Sam.

    Why? Am I driving later?

    Point taken. So, what about this Jolene? Sounds like you were building up to something.

    I was. So, it was about a week ago when Robert was in

a terrible way, and I just had to get out of there. I went home, showered, got a change of clothes, and made my way back to the hospital. Only I couldn't quite make it. I just couldn't face that building no more. I could endure the day in and day out when I was there holding Robert's bony hands. But when I finally got out of there, it became too much to return. I stayed in the parking lot for at least an hour. You must think I'm a horrible woman.

    I would never, said Sam. The second time I visited Robert, near the end, I was chain-smoking three packs a day. Every time it became too much to bear, I had to go outside just to get away from it all. I couldn't be in Robert's room for more than twenty minutes, let alone the days you spent with him.

    It doesn't change the fact that I felt broken by the whole thing, she said. Near the end of his fight with cancer I flinched. So, I waited in the car, hoping that I would have the courage to get back into that building. That's when I heard her ride up on her motorcycle.

    So, there *was* a Jolene, said Sam as Louisa put down a basket of mozzarella sticks.

Yes, there was, is, always has been, and always will be. Pardon?

Let me tell you the whole story. That might be a better way of explaining things than actually explaining them. Don't know if I could do the whole thing justice but that's where we are. Jolene rides up on her motorcycle, a wild white monster with high handlebars and a sidecar. She wore lots of road leather with angel and devil patches. She was wearing a black helmet with a visor shaped like a skull. I don't know how I knew it was her, but I knew for sure it was. Worse was she parked right beside me. I knew she was here to see Robert. I struggled out of the car, almost falling on the asphalt.

May I have a word with you? I said, marching right up to her.

She looked me up and down before taking that helmet off, letting down a river of dark red hair. We locked eyes, and I swear I was looking into the heart of the forest. I have never in my life seen a shade of green as I found in those eyes of hers. I felt like an elk that just locked eyes with a bear. It's hard to explain. Everything in my body told me to run away from this woman. As far and as fast as I could. Thankfully, my legs locked up. I was shivering in place like it was twenty below zero, but it was as hot as it was now.

You're Mary Lee. Robert's wife, she said, tucking that helmet under her arm.

I am, and we need to talk, I said as she pulled back a glove to show a watch.

We have some time for that. Mind if we go to the diner across the way?

That will work, I said to her. I was thankful that she suggested someplace where I could sit down. I don't think I could have continued that confrontation on my feet.

Should we take your car or my bike?

My car will do, I said. So, we made our way to the diner. Delilah's Diner, if it matters to you.

Good patty melts, said Sam.

I wouldn't know. Anyhow, we got into the diner and found a booth a bit like this one, and she sat across from me. To tell you what I was feeling right then and there could take all day. I guess a close way of explaining it would be like if you opened your door one day and saw a twister right out on the street. Only it snuck up on ya. That's what it was like sitting there with Jolene. A waitress came up and took our order. I think I ordered coffee. Any thought of eating went right out the window. I just wanted to get this conversation done. Not Jolene. She ordered a chocolate milkshake and asked if it came with the steel cup that it was mixed in. They did, and she gave a smile so sweet and warm it made me forget for a moment that I hated her. But only for a moment. She also asked if she could get a ramekin of maraschino cherries. Soon, it was just us with our respective drinks. I remember so clearly how she would pluck the cherry stems two at a time before tossing the cherries into the steel cup. All very deliberate and practiced.

    How do you know Robert? I finally asked her.

    I have always known him, she said.

    That don't explain nothing.

    Really? I thought it was succinct.

    How do you know Robert?

    She was very calm as she began to suck down her milkshake. I had forgotten my coffee and didn't plan on drinking it anyhow. I was starting to suspect that she was more interested in that damn milkshake than she was with me.

I have known him for a long time, much longer than you. We first met when he stepped out in traffic without looking both ways into the path of an oncoming truck. Right before his mother pulled him back onto the sidewalk. I was in the restaurant two years ago when a large chunk of beef lodged itself in his throat, only to be cleared with a glass of water. Now it's time he and I went on a trip.

He is in no condition to be taking any trips. He's got stomach cancer, I said.

He is in just the right condition for this trip.

Well, you can't have him, I said to her.

Beg your pardon? she asked, putting her milkshake down.

You heard me. You can't have him. He's my man, and I ain't gonna allow some trollop to take him away from me.

Mary Lee, that's not how this works.

Like hell it ain't, I told her. You can have any man in town. Robert is mine, and I don't plan on giving him up. Least of all to someone like yourself.

You're upset, said Jolene.

Damn straight I am, I said. She took another long sip of her milkshake, and I could see the wheels turning in her head.

Mary Lee, there is something you must understand. Robert and I have been planning this trip for a long time. It's not up to you whether Robert stays or goes. One way or another, Robert is leaving town with me. That is not up for debate.

Well, that's not right, I'm his wife. You can't just decide to take my man. You can't have him. Please don't take him. He's not well.

It looked like I had finally gotten through to her. She gave a little sigh while drinking her shake before checking her watch. Then she pulled out this day planner and began to look it over. She blew a lock of hair out of her green eyes, and the whole time she looked through that little black day planner, I held my breath.

I have a lot of other appointments I need to keep while I'm in town. I can come to get Robert when I'm done. You got a whole extra day with him. That's all I can give you.

When she said this, I knew I was beaten. But I also felt like I won. I fell back in the booth, not knowing what was up or down. She finished her milkshake and offered to pay for the coffee as well. She left several dollars on the table but wrote a date from three years from now on the tip line of the receipt.

What the hell is this? asked the waitress.

You know what it is, Jolene replied. The waitress was dumbstruck. Like a bolt of lightning had hit her. She took off her apron and shouted at her manager.

I quit! I ain't spending the rest of my days in this shit hole. I'm going to Paris. The manager was confused, and nothing that man could say could convince the waitress to return. She was out the door.

Who knows, said Jolene. You might convince him to stay. Stranger things have happened. She left the diner, got on her bike in the parking lot, and drove off.

Wait a moment, said Sam. Didn't she leave her bike at the hospital?

Spooky, right? I have been puzzling through that one all week. What's strange is what happened when I returned to the hospital. Robert was so doped up because of the pain that he really couldn't do much besides sleep. Now, he was awake, lively, and free of any pain. The doctors ran some tests while Robert and I had our first real conversation in a long while that didn't have anything to do with cancer, pain, or any of that. The doctors couldn't explain any of it. Cancer specialists said that not only was recovery like this unlikely at this stage of cancer, but it should have been impossible. I asked if I could get him checked out for the day. My reasoning was cautious. I didn't want him to make a bad turn, but I also wanted to keep Jolene from him. She said she was coming for him in a day, and I aimed to throw her off his scent.

Well, after a little pestering, I convinced them to let Robert out. He was happy to be dressed in anything besides a hospital gown. None of his clothes fit him anymore. His shirt hung off him like a gown, and his belt was at the last notch to keep his pants up.

Robert didn't want to go straight home. He wanted to drive. Given his condition, we compromised. I would drive us around town, and he would pick the direction. We drove all the rest of that day, having to refill the tank twice. We talked about nothing and everything. Everything except Jolene. When it was dark, I called the hospital and told them of Robert's condition. He was tired but doing well. They said it would be alright if he slept at the house that night, but it would be best if I brought him in the following morning. I was just so giddy that he could sleep in his own home.

    Our dinner was simple. Cheese, crackers, peanut butter, a protein smoothie, all the things that are easy to digest. I don't think there was much to say. We just ate and sat together. Our touch said more than any words could. I would have stayed up all night with Robert, but he was exhausted. Better health didn't remove cancer in his body. Afterward, we went to our bed and held each other. Not in any marital way. That just wasn't gonna happen. We fell asleep, a sleep so deep that dreams were crushed under the weight of a long day. I don't know when it was, but at some point, I awoke to find our bed empty. I thought he might have gone to the bathroom or his medical bed. I was about to roll over when I heard the revving engine of a motorcycle.

I was fully awake then. I ran out the door wearing the clothes from the day before. I didn't even put my shoes on. I just ran out into the morning dawn to see Robert sitting in Jolene's sidecar. She handed him a helmet, and when he secured it, he slapped the sidecar twice. Then they were off down the road. I called out his name as I ran after them. My bare feet slamming into the sharp asphalt. There was no way I was ever gonna catch up with them. But I chased them. I chased them until their wheels came off the road and into the sky. I collapsed and shouted after them, hoping that Robert would look back at me. He never did. He and Jolene were taking their trip, and there was nothing I could do about it. I watched them as they flew higher and higher until they disappeared in the morning sky. I cried in the middle of the street. Cried and wailed until one of my neighbors came out to check. I was gently brought home, where I found that Robert had passed in his medical bed. I can't explain what happened before that, but it was real. It happened.

    Mary Lee had slumped forward on the table, causing her glass to tip over, spilling cold beer all over. Sam grabbed the glass before it fell off the table and moved the pitcher out of her reach.

I think you've had enough to drink, he said, using a napkin to block the beer from spilling off the table.

I think you might be right, said Mary Lee, realizing she was drenched in beer.

Listen, why don't you head out to the truck? I'll pay the house, and then we can get you home. You think you can get to the truck alright?

Yeah, I can do that.

Sam paid Louisa, making sure to give her a thirty percent tip before heading out. As they drove home, Mary Lee leaned her head against the window, watching the cars and the scenery.

Nasty-looking accident, said Sam as they slowed down, following the road flairs around a turned-over sedan. Mary Lee looked over and saw the wreck, the paramedics and police there trying to put some order to the chaos of the traffic accident. As they slowly rode by, Mary Lee saw Jolene helping a young man out of the car, leading him to her bike.

A Gradient into Shadows

82

Totally Totalitarian

Monday

Malissa was given the same lecture she had always gotten when she started a new school. "Be on time, don't curse, don't draw on anything that isn't a notebook, and for Christ's sake make a friend," said her stepmother on the car ride over.

"Whatever, Lisa," she said as they got closer to Copperhead High.

"See, that's what I'm talking about. Your constant need to childishly challenge authority is going to get you in trouble. Why don't you ever call me Mom?"

"Do we have to do this right now?" asked Malissa.

"We will get back to it when you get home tonight. Now listen, this school is one of the best in the state. I think you will do great here, just don't do anything to get yourself kicked out again."

"Goodbye, Lisa," she said, exiting the car.

"Take care," said Lisa before Malissa slammed the door. Entering the school, she noticed that everyone was dressed practically the same. It wasn't long after that observation that Malissa realized there was something off about Copperhead High.

"What the fuck," whispered Malissa. It was always a bitch transferring into a new school in the middle of the year. Still, she didn't expect the utter fanaticism of school spirit at Copperhead High. Everyone was wearing the red and white fighting colors in a bewildering exultation of school spirit. She felt out of place and exposed, wearing her black gothic-punk accessories, acid-washed black jeans, and lucky *Misfits* T-shirt. It wasn't abnormal for her to look out of place. That was the goal. However, at Copperhead High, she was an obvious outsider.

It took her several minutes to locate her locker and spin the right combination. The tumblers didn't squeak or rattle. It seemed like everything in this school had an aggressive level of polish. There wasn't any graffiti on the lockers, the floors weren't scuffed, and all the lights worked.

"Like the fucking Twilight Zone," she whispered as she deposited her unneeded books in her locker. She took one of her art pens and wrote "Goth life" inside her locker with a couple skulls thrown in for good measure.

"Oh, my goodness, what are you doing?" said a girl running up to her in a crude red and white hand-woven sweater.

"I'm bringing some character to this school, what does it look like?" said Malissa, capping her pen.

"Never mind that, where are your colors?"

"My what?"

"Your colors! It's spirit week and the C.H.I.P.S. are everywhere! You're going to be in big trouble with Lilly!" whispered the girl as she fumbled with her glasses.

"I just got here, I don't give a shit about any school pride, for real," she said, slamming her locker and walking off.

"Wait!" said the girl following her. "Are you new? Oh goodness, you don't know. Could you wait one sec?" Malissa sighed while the girl rummaged around in her backpack. "You're lucky I always keep a backup sweater. This should get you through the day," she said, handing Malissa the red and white garment as the first morning bell rang. "Crap, I wish I had time to explain. Listen, my name is Aubrey."

"Malissa."

"Meet me at lunch in the cafeteria and try not to draw any attention to yourself. Just blend in," said Aubrey before running off.

"Wait! What do you mean...shit," she said as the girl vanished in the crowd. She looked at the sweater in her hands. It read "Lilly Turner for Class President" with a crudely knitted red snake below it.

"This is the most godawful thing I have ever seen," said Malissa as she stuffed the sweater into her bag. The hallways cleared out in no time, leaving Malissa to wander the halls until she found herself late for class. When she finally found her room, she was given a red binder with the class's reference material and a desk in the back of the class. While the teacher broke down math formulas, Malissa examined the course material. All the basic stuff she had covered at her old school. But what caught her attention was the folded note with aggressively elegant calligraphy addressed to her.

> Dear Malissa,
> Welcome to Copperhead High. I am certain you will make a wonderful addition to my student body. I have reviewed your school records and am pleased you have excellent grades, a sure sign of intelligence that would be well suited to any of our school's clubs or even as an assistant to the student body government. Unlike the other dirty, disorganized schools you have attended, Copperhead High prides itself on having an active student culture. I think it will be important for you to find your place quickly so as not to cause any disturbances in the school's carefully orchestrated harmonics. As a result, I have taken an interest in you. I will help you in this tumultuous transition from chaos to unity. I can't wait for us to finally meet after school.

Your President,

Lilly Turner.

P.S. It shows you have a history of delinquency, truancy, and tardiness. It is important that you arrive at class and events on time. Punctuality is a school virtue. As I say, "Better an hour early than a minute late."

Malissa crumpled the note up and tossed it into the trash, unaware that her actions were being watched and cataloged by her fellow students. The rest of the morning's classes passed in a sleepy, confusing daze. The usual disorientation of navigating the school's layout was made worse by the omnipresence of school spirit posters. The walls were covered in posters of a single blonde cheerleader embossed with a brutalist font proclaiming "Lilly leads the charge!" "Lilly Turner, highest G.P.A. in the state!" "Swearing and cursing upsets Lilly," "A clean school is a happy Lilly," "Lilly wants you! To Join the C.H.I.P.S.! Applicants need to be members of a school club or have special permission from the Student Government." There was hardly a bulletin board that didn't have at least a dozen of these posters. Malissa ignored them the best she could, but the ubiquitous nature of the school's propaganda made it difficult.

The cafeteria was filled with the same energy as the hallways. A red copperhead snake mascot strutted by tables giving students high fives. Everyone ate their food in a precise, militaristic fashion. Malissa picked the closest table that had an available seat.

"Can I sit here?" she asked, placing her brown sack lunch down. The students at the table looked her over, scowled, and left without a word.

"What the hell?" said Malissa, sitting at the empty table. She didn't stink or anything, so she chalked it up to a bit of hazing of the new kid. She pulled out her pens and began to doodle on the cafeteria table.

"Thank goodness I found you. Why aren't you wearing the sweater I gave you?" asked Aubrey with a carefully balanced school lunch.

"It's not my style," she said, gesturing to her *Misfits* shirt.

"Listen, you must put that sweater on before the

C.H.I.P.S. spot you. They might have already documented it," said Aubrey as she rummaged around her backpack.

"Hey, what's the deal with this place? This table had a bunch of people at it and they left as soon as I sat down. What gives?"

"You're not wearing your colors. If people are seen with you, they could get kicked out of their school club, or worse. Ah ha! Found it," said Aubrey as she pulled out a pair of red and white hair bands. Suddenly, like shadows peeling out of the crowd, two boys in identical shirts, pants, and Copperhead High armbands sat at the table.

"Nice looking lunch, misfit," said one of the boys.

"Cafeteria food not good enough for you?" said the other.

"Must think it's art class with how much she's drawn on the table."

"Not enough school spirit either."

"What the fuck is happening?" said Malissa.

"Who's your friend, Aubrey?"

"She's got a bit of a potty mouth."

"President Turner is not going to like that."

"Andrew, Ryan, she's new to the school, I'm just trying to help her fit in," said Aubrey, shrinking from the boys. "I was trying to get her to wear some school flair," she said, holding up the hair bands.

"Sounds like a worthy cause, don't you think, Andrew?" said the boy next to Aubrey.

"Mighty worthy, maybe worthy of privileges."

"We could put that in our report, tell Lilly all the good work Aubrey is doing."

"The only problem is we are fresh out of paper, and paper can be expensive."

"I have cash to buy paper!" Aubrey whimpered as she pulled out her bag and put some bills on the table.

"Aubrey, you don't have to give in to these assholes," said Malissa, putting her hand on Aubrey's money.

"Shut your mouth, misfit, or we'll shut it for you," said the boy next to Malissa.

"Malissa, please, you don't need to worry," Aubrey's eyes were pleading and scared. Malissa understood and took her hand off the money. "I think the members of the C.H.I.P.S. should have the best paper on the market," said Aubrey, putting more money on the table.

"Your donations to the morality arm of the Student Government are appreciated and accepted," said Ryan, and like a stone in the ocean, the boys vanished into the crowd.

"Jesus Christ, what is the deal with this school? Who the fuck are those creeps?" asked Malissa, leaning forward in a whisper.

"The Copperhead High Investigative Pep Squad. They are Lilly's eyes and ears in the school. They are always on the lookout for any moral degeneracy or signs of less than enthusiastic support for the school."

"How is this allowed?"

"They are part of the school's spirit club that organizes all school activities. That club organizes all the student events that help get everyone motivated for sports events. We win lots of games, so the teachers and principal look the other way," said Aubrey.

"That's insane."

"I know it is. That's why you need to at least put these hairbands on, so they won't harass us again. Normally all you need is some red and white on your outfit, but this is homecoming week. The C.H.I.P.S. take their duties very seriously during homecoming week. So please, put them on."

"What happens if I don't."

"If you were a boy, they might beat you up. Most likely they will hand you over to the cheerleaders for public humiliation."

"Jesus Christ, what kind of school did I walk into?" said Malissa, taking the hair bands and tying her dyed black hair.

"Lilly Turner's school."

"Well, that explains everything," Malissa said, rolling her eyes. "So, who the fuck is Lilly Turner anyway? I keep seeing posters of her everywhere, and I can make the guess she is the leader of the student government, and I think a cheerleader or whatever, and she has her own squad of spies or some shit. It's fucking weird."

"Don't speak so loudly, and for heaven's sake, don't curse!" whispered Aubrey. "It's just the way it is, Malissa. Lilly is a Senior, and from what I heard, she reorganized the school as a freshman. Before Lilly, we didn't win any school games, football, basketball, debate, nothing. But then she started using her personal touch, and we started winning. After that, she had the full support of the jocks, the cheerleaders, then the school government, and her influence trickled down to the rest of us. There isn't a place in this school that isn't in some way influenced or organized by Lilly. The best thing you can do is to go with the flow."

"Fuck that. I know Lilly's type; she is just a mean girl with a modicum of power. I didn't take shit from her type back in McGeary High and I'm not going to let her boss me around, she can just take that letter she sent me and stuff it."

"You got a letter from Lilly?" asked Aubrey. "Show it to me!"

"I can't, I threw it away, it was just a weird welcome letter," said Malissa.

"We need to go to your locker right now," said Aubrey, getting up.

"Right now? I just started eating lunch."

"Lunch can wait," said Aubrey as she slung her bag over her shoulder and dumped her lunch in the trash.

"Jesus Christ, why does every high school I go to have to be so fucking dramatic?" said Malissa as she took her sack lunch and followed Aubrey to her locker. The hallway was empty except for a few students running errands at lunch. Malissa turned the locker dial to the proper combination and opened it up. Absent was the graffiti Malissa had made earlier, as someone had quickly cleaned it when she was gone. Atop her books was the crumpled letter with the same aggressively elegant calligraphy.

"What the hell! I thought I threw that away."

"Nothing of Lilly's ever gets thrown away," said Aubrey as she read the note. She reread it while leaning on the lockers. She reread it as she slowly sank to the floor.

"What's so important about that letter?" asked Malissa.

"Lilly doesn't send letters. She does proclamations," said Aubrey as tears rolled down her face.

"Hey, what's going on?" said Malissa, sitting beside Aubrey. The girl wiped her cheek before suddenly embracing

Malissa. Malissa awkwardly patted Aubrey's back as her classmate sobbed into her *Misfits* T-shirt.

"She wants you for some reason, and I'm afraid Lilly is going to take you away from me. I know we just met but I thought we were going to be friends. Real friends! Not like my friends from the sewing club. They aren't my friends. They are my jailers. Everyone is everyone's jailer here."

"It's going to be alright, Aubrey. We can still be friends," she said.

"I wish that were true," said Aubrey as she took her glasses off to wipe her eyes. "I must look so pathetic, but you are the only person at school that doesn't have Lilly's stamp all over her."

"You're not pathetic. It sucks having fake friends and being alone," said Malissa as she opened her sack lunch. "Here's half a sandwich and an apple. It looks like you didn't eat anything before throwing your lunch away."

"Thanks," said Aubrey as she bit into the sandwich. The lunch was reported, documented, analyzed, cataloged, and judged.

Malissa was exhausted after a long, confusing day of organizing her schedule to catch up with her peers. It didn't help that she always felt like she was being watched. At her old school, her fashion and attitude made her seem aggressive and forgettable. Just the weird goth-punk girl that you see every so often. Not here. She stood out in a sea of red and white. The hairbands kept her from getting hassled by the C.H.I.P.S., but she was not fitting in. Before she could pack up and leave school, Ryan grabbed her bag.

"It's time to meet with President Turner," he said.

"Give me my fucking bag back, asshole!" said Malissa, reaching for her bag only for the C.H.I.P.S. member to pull it out of her reach.

"You will get it back after you meet with President Turner."

"Fine," she said, following Ryan to the Student Government office. They opened the door, and the smell of vanilla espresso and cinnamon wafted out. The room had several long tables in a horseshoe pattern. A dozen students were cataloging pictures and notes and pinning them to large cork bulletin boards that read "Yearbook Organization Committee."

A student in the corner was playing a dark red cello. At the center of the room, sipping from a porcelain white cup and dressed in her cheerleader's uniform, was Lilly Turner. Her long blond hair had the look of meticulous brushing and combing. Her makeup was a subtle punctuation to the sentence that was her face. With closed eyes, she took a deep breath, inhaling the steaming espresso before taking a sip. With a gratified smile, she placed the cup on a napkin beside a blood-handled pair of scissors. Lilly opened her eyes to meet Malissa.

"Enchanté...Malissa."

"I don't speak French," said Malissa.

"Few people at our wonderful school do," said Lilly, taking another sip from her cup. "Ryan, Andrew, get Malissa a chair and something to drink."

"I'm not thirsty."

Lilly smiled as the C.H.I.P.S. brought her a chair while the others began to work at the hissing espresso machine in the corner. In no time at all, Malissa was sitting across from Lilly with an identical steaming cup of coffee in front of her. Malissa kept her arms crossed and rocked back in her chair.

"Balancing on the backs of chairs is a safety violation," said Lilly.

"Call the cops," said Malissa.

"That won't be necessary," smiled Lilly. "We will get that attitude sorted out soon enough."

"Look, whatever this is"—Malissa gestured to the room— "I don't want any part of it. From what I can tell, you're just a spoiled bitch living out her weird power fantasies by bullying the rest of the school. I'm not playing your fucked-up game." The cellist and yearbook drones stopped working. For a heartbeat, there was total silence. Expressions of horror and pity covered the faces of everyone in the room except for Lilly, whose face was beatific and gentle.

"I really hate profanity," said Lilly. "It's so vulgar, so unbecoming for a member of our school. Marcus, please keep playing. Bach if you will, Cello Suite No. 1, Prelude. The buzzing has gotten loud today." Marcus started up again, and the yearbook drones returned to work.

"Buzzing?" asked Malissa.

"Yes, buzzing, like a swarm of bees flying around in your skull. You see, Malissa, out in the world all I hear is buzzing. People claim they don't hear it, but I know that they do. It's why the world is so crazy. Everyone hears that buzzing and it drives them insane. In my freshman year, there was so much buzzing I couldn't think. My thoughts were drowned out by it, so I had to do something. So, I did. Bit by bit, once I became head cheerleader and then president of the student body government, the buzzing began to fade, and I could finally think clearly. I can finally get some peace."

"That's insane. Can I leave now?"

"Not yet. Ryan would you be so kind," said Lilly as the C.H.I.P.S. brought over Malissa's bag before browsing its contents.

"What are you doing? That's my shit!" said Malissa as she lunged for the bag. Andrew had crept behind her and pulled her back into her seat.

"Let's see, textbooks, sketchbook, homework, MP3 player, no doubt filled with punk and goth. The pens that have been defiling my lockers and cafeteria tables, and a sweater.

"Hmm, very poor stitching, looks like Aubrey's work," said Lilly.

"Aubrey tried to bribe several C.H.I.P.S. officers earlier today," said Ryan.

"What! That's bullshit, these assholes were the ones that asked for the bribe," said Malissa.

"We followed the standard protocol of exposing insincere club students, Madam President."

"Well, she will have to be punished," said Lilly, standing up and grabbing the pair of blood-handled scissors.

"She didn't do anything wrong!"

"Aubrey has been on thin ice for a while, Malissa. She has been known to cry in the bathroom and not engage fully in sewing club activities. Not to mention the constant spread of lies about the student government to new students. She is going to be dealt with. Later. As for you—Andrew, Ryan…" The pair of C.H.I.P.S. simultaneously grabbed Malissa and dragged her to the center of the room.

"Get off me, you bastards!" she shouted as she kicked and struggled against them.

"Malissa, right now you are the loudest buzzing in my school. You are intelligent, passionate, and I think you will make a great addition to my staff as my aide. But you wear your rebelliousness out in the open, right on your shirt. I must do what's necessary to maintain harmony in this school."

Lilly took the scissors and began to cut away the *Misfits* T-shirt. Each cut elicited screams of anguish and blubbering tears from Malissa. Lilly cut until the shirt was in ribbons, and it took no effort for Andrew and Ryan to rip it from her body. Malissa cried as the two C.H.I.P.S. stepped back, leaving Malissa in her bra, crying in the center of the room. Lilly crouched down and embraced Malissa. She recoiled. Lilly cooed and shushed Malissa as she cried.

"Shhhhhh, sweet bright girl. Can you hear it? The buzzing is dying down. It's OK, my sweet darling Malissa. We will get through this together. Just you and me. You don't have to be alone anymore. If you follow my rules, you will be happy and content."

"Why are you doing this? I hate you. I hate you!" shouted Malissa.

"No, you don't, you are just afraid of what you will become," whispered Lilly. "The cocoon of your transformation is a dark and scary place. But when you emerge, I will be there to witness your beautiful wings," the two rocked in place while Lilly cooed in Malissa's ear. They rocked for so long that Malissa's cries died down to an occasional sniffle.

"Andrew, get Malissa her sweater. I don't want her to catch a cold."

"Yes, Madam President," said Andrew as he passed the sweater to Lilly.

"Thank you. Now Malissa. One arm at a time, that's a good girl. I knew you would look good in our school's colors; all that black made you look so gloomy. Now, I don't want to have to repeat this incident. I want a prominent display of school spirit."

"Yes, Lilly."

"That's a good girl. Ryan, why don't you drive Malissa back home? She's had a big day after all. The first day at a new school can be such a scary and exhausting time."

Malissa returned home in a fog. She knew she sat in the

back of Ryan's car and that he brought her back to her home. How he knew her home address was not a question she asked until late that night when she found herself shaking with the realization that Lilly somehow knew. The cello played in her head as she desperately sought sleep. A sleep that passed in the blink of an eye.

That morning, she looked through her wardrobe of black clothes. Band T-shirts hung above acid-stained black jeans and black leather boots. The closest thing she had to school colors was a red and black plaid skirt she had worn once and stuffed in the back of her closet.

"You need to go shopping for school clothes. This wardrobe doesn't have enough school spirit," she thought. A moment later, Malissa gasped and put a hand to her mouth. The voice in her head wasn't her own but Lilly's delicate voice. She focused on dressing, ensuring her black shirt was fully covered by the "Vote for Lilly Turner" sweater Aubrey had made.

Aubrey's face came into her head, and she remembered how Lilly said she needed to be punished. Malissa had to warn Aubrey. She was nearly frantic when she arrived at school.

There weren't many students at this early hour, but she went and questioned everyone she saw.

"Have you seen Aubrey? She is a little shorter than me, part of the sewing club?"

"Sorry never heard of her," said the early students in the halls. Malissa finally found the sewing club and a few people knitting and crocheting red and white clothes.

"I'm looking for Aubrey, I think she is in trouble," said Malissa, out of breath.

"Aubrey? Never heard of her," said the club leader.

"What? That's bull...crap...I know she is part of this club!" said Malissa.

"We have never had a club member named Aubrey. Lilly made it clear we have never had a member named Aubrey," said the club leader. "Isn't that right, sewing club!" she said, turning to the few girls working before class.

"Never heard of her," they said in unison.

"What the...crap?" yelled Malissa.

Malissa stormed out and made her way to the student government office. But before she could barge in, the smell of vanilla espresso and cinnamon hit her nose, making her weak in the knees.

Lilly was sitting at the head of the horseshoe while her army of yearbook drones worked around her. She sipped her coffee while several C.H.I.P.S. showed her documents, photos, and rumors.

"Malissa," smiled Lilly, waving the C.H.I.P.S. away. "It's going to be a wonderful day, don't you think?"

"Shut the...heck up Lilly! What happened to Aubrey!" shouted Malissa. The C.H.I.P.S. began to move in on Malissa, anger and hate contorting their faces.

"It's quite alright, boys," said Lilly with a raised hand. The C.H.I.P.S. retreated into the shadows.

"Now, Malissa, who is Aubrey?" she asked.

"Aubrey! From the sewing club! My friend!" shouted Malissa as she slammed her fists on Lilly's table.

"I'm afraid no one named Aubrey goes to this school, I don't think an Aubrey has ever gone to this school," smiled Lilly.

"Bull crap! I'm wearing her sweater right now! She

gave this to me to protect me from your...jerk bodyguards!"

A corner of Lilly's mouth twitched for the briefest moment. Her smile remained, and Lilly threw her steaming hot coffee onto Malissa with the quickest flick of her wrists. Malissa recoiled and screamed as the hot liquid scalded her. The heat clung to her as the liquid soaked into her clothes and scorched her skin.

"Malissa, you clumsy girl, you spilled my coffee all over yourself," said Lilly, passing her cup to get it refilled by an aid. Malissa hissed as her skin grew a pink-red that stung to touch.

"Oh, and your sweater is covered in coffee, it's going to leave a stain. You better give it to me to get it washed up before lunch," said Lilly as the C.H.I.P.S. surrounded Malissa.

"Please no, you can't take this sweater from me," whispered Malissa.

"I insist," said Lilly, grabbing the same, red-handled scissors from yesterday. Malissa realized what was about to happen and began to shake in place. Flashes of yesterday's humiliation swirled through her head. Malissa mechanically removed her sweater and handed it to Andrew, who towered over her.

"Don't worry, Malissa, we will have your sweater cleaned up by lunch. Now, what was it we were talking about? Your friend Aubrey?" said Lilly, snipping the scissors closed.

"Who…" gulped Malissa. "Who's Aubrey?"

"I don't know, Malissa. Never heard of her. Now you better get to class, you have a big day ahead of you, lots to learn, and I want you ready when you work as my assistant this evening."

Malissa went to class, unable to focus at all. The words in her head droned on and on about sitting up straight and not rocking in her chair, all in Lilly's voice. It was like Lilly was clipping away the distasteful parts of her as one clips the errant twig of a bonsai tree. At lunch, Andrew returned a sweater to Malissa. Still, it was clear from the careful pristine stitching that it wasn't the sweater Aubrey had given her.

"Who is Aubrey?" thought Malissa in Lilly's voice. "Never heard of her."

Friday

Homecoming was Lilly's crowning achievement. It was complete with all the pomp and circumstance the school could muster. All week Malissa watched as Copperhead High waged a war against its regional rival South Ogden High. Humiliations and threats were sent to rival players while the cheerleader squad set up impromptu routines in the cafeteria to raise the fighting spirit of the student body. Special commando squads raided Ogden High, kidnapping mascots, slashing the tires of the team's school bus, and sabotaging essential training equipment. All the while, the C.H.I.P.S. stalked the halls of Copperhead High, ever vigilant for any signs of waning spirit or subversive thoughts, and disappearing any student found wanting. On game day, the visitors' section of Ogden High was a small crowd hemmed in by the roaring fanatics of Copperhead High.

The school's mania took hold of Malissa. She booed at the visitors' pitiful show of school spirit while her school lock-stepped in perfect harmony. The visitors were a dirty, disorganized lot with mismatched clothing that barely contained the green and black of Ogden High's colors. Their mascot, a haggard frumpy bear, lacked any of the majesty and fighting spirit of the Copperhead. Malissa found it easy to hate them, and Lilly made it easy to hate them.

Malissa occasionally glanced at Lilly, who led the cheer squad front and center. Malissa was grateful to sit on the cheerleaders' bench to watch the game with her clipboard, which helped organize Lilly's schedule. Malissa was entranced by Lilly's performance. Her cheers and gestures could elicit roars of approval and steadfast devotion to Copperhead High. Lilly was the conductor of a symphony that was the school's pride and the crown jewel of the whole affair.

Malissa was overcome with emotion when the cheerleading squad raised Lilly high in the air like a shooting star at the top of a pyramid of red and white human bricks. Tears ran down Malissa's face as Lilly raised her pom-pom high in the sky in the ultimate display of dominant magnificence. The crowd roared as Lilly returned to earth, ending the cheerleader's routine.

"President Turner, that was amazing!" blubbered Malissa as she gave her president a bottle of chilled espresso. "This homecoming is so wonderful and it's all thanks to you."

"I couldn't have done it without you, Malissa. Today is perfect," said Lilly as she looked over the roaring crowd. "You have been invaluable to me this entire week of preparation."

"Oh, don't say that. I just did what you asked," said Malissa shyly.

"I'm serious, Malissa, you are my crowning achievement. I couldn't have pulled this off without you. I can safely say that I'm leaving Copperhe—"

"Please rise for our National Anthem!" said the stadium announcer, leading the crowd to go quiet and turn to the American flag. There was no one to lead the crowd, and so an impromptu singing from Ogden High spread like wildfire through the Copperhead fans.

"What is happening?" whispered Lilly as her fists began to shake angrily.

"What's wrong?" asked Malissa, in a fearful blubber.

"That! That is what's wrong!" shouted Lilly as she pointed at the American flag. "I finally got the buzzing to stop and that caused it to flare up again louder than ever! I can't…

my day...my school...everything is being ruined!"

"Ryan! Andrew!" shouted Malissa as the two C.H.I.P.S. appeared from nowhere. "Ryan, you get that flag off that pole and run up the school's flag! Andrew, I need you to get in the announcer's booth and play a recording of our school's fight song," The C.H.I.P.S. looked at each other and then at Lilly.

"Do it," shouted Lilly, and the two vanished to carry out their respective missions. Before the "rocket's red glare" was uttered, Copperhead's fight song erupted from the stadium speakers. The supporters of Ogden High began to boo as the American flag was lowered off the flagpole, only to be replaced by the hissing snake flag of Copperhead High. Lilly's anger and fury died down as Copperhead's larger crowd began to chant the school's fight song, drowning out the boos of Ogden High. Lilly smiled with contentment, and she began to weep, her tears marring her delicate makeup. The other cheerleaders gasped and retreated, averting their gaze at the crying Lilly. Only Malissa remained by Lilly's side.

"President Turner...why are you...you know...?"

"Crying?" said Lilly as she watched the fluttering of the

school's flag. "I'm crying because this will be my last homecoming. I have been accepted into Yale. A steppingstone for my political career. But I was afraid all my hard work here would be undone. That the buzzing in me would return, leaving me no place of solace in this wide world," she said, turning to Malissa and taking her by the shoulders. "You are everything I could have ever wanted in a successor. I need you to keep this place quiet and serene for me, while I go out and stop the buzzing in the rest of the world."

"I don't know if I can, I'm not strong enough, President Turner."

"To all others, I am President Turner; for you my sweet, beautiful Malissa, it's Lilly."

"Lilly I...I don't know if I can."

"You can. A minute ago, you acted with decisive efficiency while I found myself in a moment of weakness. I now know that our school will be left in safe hands, while I sort out the chaos of the rest of the world."

"I'm honored in your faith in me," said Malissa. Lilly took a deep breath, wiped the tears away, and embraced Malissa.

"We still have a whole school year to get you ready, before I have to start all over in the big leagues."

"If anyone can stop the buzzing it's you, Lilly!" said Malissa.

"You can hear it?"

"Of course, Lilly, it's almost deafening."

A Gradient into Shadows

The Wild Hunt

The Prince of Summer's Eve was stricken with boredom, a condition first noted by the seneschal of the Court of Knives. He quipped that the Prince was not very enthusiastic during the festival of laurels. Naturally, the other members of the gentry thought that it was some subtle machination, a form of politics of a higher order, and beyond understanding. However, as the endless days and nights passed, the Prince's lovers, both secret and known began to lament that the Prince's enthusiasm had waned. They wept in the gardens of morning that his vigor was absent and his attention fleeting.

The servants began to openly gossip that the Prince

would spend all his days and nights in bed. How he could be found crawling around the palace like a slug, his antlers gouging great furrows in the earth. When he ate tarts and wild game, he would chew like a cow. His clothes became like a dreary bog, absent any of the dazzle meant to delight his peers in court. His duties were also neglected, as the wyrdstones that kept any outsiders from sneaking into Fairy were falling into disrepair. Only the blood of the Prince could mend these stones. There were even whispers that a band of Reavers had already broken into Fairy, but that would be dealt with once the Prince's mood was lightened.

So, the court did what it always did in a crisis. They threw a feast. The forest contorted and twisted into a central chamber of a magnificent ballroom. The branches of towering trees grew upward before intertwining their willowy limbs to create a vaulted roof. The gnomes of the stone cutters guild went into action and made a dance floor from river stones. The stones were fitted so perfectly that a playing card could not be squeezed between them. The Court of Flowers scoured all of Fairy for the most exotic flowers to decorate the chamber.

They found thistle blooms, twilight tulips, and long funneled darkling mushrooms. Carnivorous shimmer blossoms were carried with care while thin vines of suckle cups were made into crowns. Even a singing fern was flattered into joining the festivities.

While the craftsmen of Fairy sweated, the Court of Summer's Eve began to move with all the alacrity of their caste. The court's seneschal called in every favor he had, and the most eligible bachelors and maidens of Fairy were invited. Nymphs with dresses of velvet leaves arrived with bawdy satyrs following behind. Heiferkin played their drums of horn and leather while tundra pixies sang in tune with their curved harps. Meadow brownies and autumn dryads laughed with delight at each other's choice of fashion. The dawn sisters scoffed at the advances of the silver suiters while hog fellows rolled in their caskets of beer and wine that they had been saving for a special occasion. All the well-to-do Fair Folk vowed to make a token appearance to the event of the season.

While the gentry played their game of words, the cooks of the court began the undertaking of their careers. The wizened cooks of the Paunch spared no expense for the finest ingredients. The cooks made haunting glass sculptures from the sugar daggers of Ool. Game hens were stuffed with nuts and sweet grass. Hundreds of platters of vibrant-jam-filled pastries were prepared, while a legion of goblins slaved over boiling caldrons of roiling soup, mulled wines, and the cook's laundry. The goblins would howl with laughter whenever an inattentive comrade fell into one of the boiling pots. At the center of the feast was the Prince's favorite dish. A wild stag's heart, eaten raw with bare hands.

    The court's jubilation seemed to bubble in the hearts of all of Fairy. Many didn't expect to see another feast of its equal for many moons. But in all the excitement, there was one who had his doubts. The Court Jester Collywak suspected that their efforts were all for naught. None were so attuned to the Prince's mercurial moods than the four-armed Collywak.

    On the eve of the feast, Collywak shuddered in silence. He knew the Prince's boredom was a great abyss, and something extraordinary would be needed to raise him out of that darkness.

The day of the feast began, and the ballroom floor was put to the test. Hundreds of fairies of all sizes danced with a passion not seen in ages. A drinking contest between satyrs and trolls spread to the entire court. A savage melee between small Fae took place in the branches of the ballroom. The brawls turned into savage duels as they ran needles and thorns into their small bodies, their blood raining down on the delighted celebrants. Gentry and servants changed roles on a whim so that all could engage in the festivities.

Lurid dances of seduction erupted like dawn roses in front of the Prince, while innumerable suitors beseeched him for an evening's delight. But the Prince's attention was on the stag's heart he held in his bare hand; he nibbled it with little enthusiasm. The Prince was served the sweetest and headiest wines which dribbled out the sides of his mouth. Eventually, he tossed the stag's heart aside and slumped on the table in apathy as his suitors played with the velvet of his antlers. Several of the members of the court approached Collywak with eyes of panic.

"What do we do?" they whispered. "The Prince's mood

has gotten worse. We have made the most valiant effort, but nothing seems to work!"

"I have put much thought into this problem," Collywak said to the crowd. "If there is one thing I know about the Prince, he delights in surprises and gifts. The ball must go on, while we procure the rarest and most exotic presents."

With this mission, fairy agents were sent across the realm. The Prince was shown the most exquisite gifts. The Thieves of Twilight procured a bolt of sunlight that was woven into a coat by the Guild of Garments. The Prince stripped himself nude, much to the delight of the court, before donning the coat. He ran his hands over the soft texture, before his attention was diverted for a moment by a fetching satyr, the shimmering coat forgotten.

A rare bottle of gloom berry wine was given to the Prince by the Caliph of Arachnids. The vintage was infused with the venom of hundreds of spiders, a powerful kick to an equally powerful wine. The Prince drained the bottle, burped, and tossed it aside. Wine dribbled down on his glowing coat of sunlight. He politely thanked the Caliph before slumping back down on the table.

Woodlock the great hunter stepped from the shadows with a mischievous smile. A hush came over the festival as Woodlock was known to bring the rarest of game. The hunter placed a swaddled babe before the royal Prince, and for a moment the Prince was intrigued.

"What is this creature, brave hunter?" asked the Prince as he picked up the mewling infant.

"It is a human child, my lord."

"I have not heard of such a thing. I know you only go after the most dangerous game, yet this creature seems pathetic."

"At first glance, my lord, but it will grow into a cunning and violent creature."

"It grows? How large?" asked the Prince.

"Maybe a head taller than yourself my lord. These creatures are prone to violent outbursts. They have a myriad of strange customs. Given a few dozen seasons, it will be a most dangerous prey."

The babe began to whimper as the Prince turned it over

in his hands. The child let out an ear-splitting wail. The party stopped in its tracks. Everyone but the Prince and Woodlock held their ears.

"What is this wailing, brave hunter? It pains my ears worse than a mandrake root."

"It is afraid, my lord. This noise drives humans into a frenzy. I barely kept my skin intact once the human warriors found I had taken the child."

The Prince grimaced. He took a drop of wine from his goblet and placed it in the child's mouth. The babe then fell silent and slept. Then a fowl stench erupted from the child's bottom.

"It's putrid!" cried the Prince, handing the child off to Collywak.

"A defense against larger animals from feasting on it. Eventually, it will learn how to control it."

"I thank you for this gift. I will feel the joy of restraint as it grows," sighed the Prince. Collywak was disturbed as the Prince sank deeper into his boredom. He ordered that the festival should continue. Gentry and servants were rotated in and out of the ballroom, whose floors were now cracked and chipped. The Court of Flowers was driven into exhaustion as they kept the festivities stocked with fresh flowers. The cooks worked night and day, providing more ingenious sauces and desserts for the feast, while they took turns sleeping on the hard floors of the kitchen. All the while, a cavalcade of gifts and surprises were brought before the Prince. All these presents were thrown carelessly into a growing pile of rare and exotic goods.

The lovers of the Prince came to Collywak with a plan to embarrass and rouse his choler. Collywak nodded in approval as he worked out his plan.

Lyla Crimson, the moth-winged Flutterkin, the most haughty and jealous of the Prince's lovers, took her position across from Desdemona Dark, her chief rival, and the most scandalous fairy in court. Their plan was simple and elegant, as they would confront each other and start a brawl for the Prince's affections. The scandal would surely rouse the Prince from his apathy.

The brawl started innocently enough; a curt remark here, a poignant barb there. This led to splashes of wine, slaps to the face, the tearing of clothes, biting, kicking, and brawling. The dancing in the ball stopped as the Prince's lovers fought in earnest. Many Fae were moved to tears as the two lovers sacrificed their reputations in the valiant attempt to lift the Prince's spirits. Others laughed at the lurid spectacle and cheered for greater violence and bloodshed.

The Prince's attention slowly drifted to the brawling rivals in the center of the dance floor. He sighed, and with a slouching shuffle, made his way to a punch bowl. He picked the bowl up and splashed his two lovers with the burgundy juice. The fight was over as the two sputtered and coughed. The Prince dropped the punch bowl and returned to his seat at the head of the feast table and tried to balance a spoon on his nose.

The Fair Folk's kingdom was in an uproar. No one knew what to do about the crisis. The kingdom was without any simple delights as all were procured for the endless feast. The ball was a vortex that sucked all the life out of Fairy. All the while, the situation with the band of human Reavers grew worse. They came up the rivers riding strange boats and were depriving fairies of their goods and lives. Everyone knew that the only solution to the crises was to somehow cure the Prince's languor. All the people of Fairy turned to Collywak.

"I have a performance," said Collywak.

"Then you must do it!" The Fae cried.

"It is still a little unpolished," said Collywak.

"The kingdom is at stake!"

"Then I shall," bowed Collywak with a flourish of his hat. "Bring me the human babe."

While Collywak made his preparations, the Reavers floated up the river on their boats. They were savage, hard men with steely eyes that glared at the exaggerated splendor of Fairy. At their head was their War Leader, a woman who had never seen Fairy, who as a girl longed to see the beauty of this realm. She wanted to dance with the inhabitants and get lost in the innumerable delights. Now she only saw the inhabitants of Fairy with eyes of hatred. They floated on their boats toward the endless celebration.

"My lord Prince, I have something special for you this evening," said Collywak, bringing forth a red-curtained castelet decorated with thistle flowers.

"Oh?" said the Prince, resting his head in a pudding.

"It might be my finest work," said Collywak with a smile. "I perform at your pleasure."

"Proceed," said the Prince with a shrug. Collywak stepped into the castelet, and the curtains rose on a puppet show. The plot of the show was novel for Fairy, as two puppets took turns beating each other over the head. Laughter roared across the ball. Fae held each other up to keep from falling over. Drunken fairies rolled on the floor unable to stand. This was the finest work of comedy that any Fae had ever seen. A joy heightened as the Prince sat up with interest. A hint of a smile came across his face. A pause in the performance allowed the ballroom to catch its breath. From behind the castelet's curtain, the mewling, teary-eye babe emerged. Chuckles erupted from the Fae at the sight of the round creature. The puppets began to hit the baby with tiny wooden clubs, causing the Fae to lose themselves with laughter. The Fae fell on the ground, holding their stomachs as the babe squealed in distress. A small smile grew on the Prince's face, and to the delight of all, he emitted a chuff of laughter.

So distracted was the court that they did not notice the Reavers entering the ballroom. Their hard eyes furrowed as they saw the laughing fairies. Their grip on their weapons tightened in rage. The War Leader's eyes locked on the puppets smacking her child. In a language considered guttural by the Fae, the War Leader spoke.

"Get my son away from these wicked creatures. Then kill them all."

The Reavers nodded and began hacking at the finely dressed Fae. Cold iron split open heads and cut open bellies. Spears pierced ribs, and swords swung wild like butcher's cleavers. Like a sudden storm, the mirth of the ball turned to terror. The Fair Folk ran in all directions in a desperate stampede to escape the Reavers' blades. The Prince was stunned by the sudden onslaught of violence. A peculiar feeling of icy terror ran up his body, from the tip of his cloven toes to the point of his antlers. He did not like this sudden surprise.

Collywak ceased his performance and raised his head to see the commotion. The babe wailed even above the carnage and slaughter. The War Leader plodded toward the perplexed

Collywak, killing everything in her wake. Collywak raised his arms in protest as the War Leader stabbed him in the chest.

"What have you done!" shouted the Prince as he watched the jester fall dead. The War Leader took her child into her arms and shouted in her guttural language. The Reavers finished their bloody acts and retreated from the ballroom, the wailing babe's lamentations growing quiet as they left. The Prince was left with the carnage of the festival. Fae of all stations were left dead or dying. The Prince watched as the fairies of the court pulled themselves to their feet. Servants from other quarters of the palace came rushing in aghast at the sights and doing what they could for the survivors. All eyes eventually turned to the Prince, who could only hold Collywak's body.

"My lord, what do we do?" asked a goblin.

"We must seek retribution," said the Prince, standing with Collywak in his arms. "These outsiders have murdered Fae in a time of celebration and slain the greatest entertainer of Fairy. Save the wounded, bury the dead. I will go and prepare for the coming storm."

The Prince left with Collywak in his arms. He wandered the forest till he found a most serene tree. He placed the body on the earth, before tearing off the golden coat and draping it over the jester's body. Vines grew up from the ground, covering the corpse before blossoming into an array of multi-colored flowers. The Prince stripped off his finery as he went deeper into the woods to the darkest depths of Fairy. He walked past spiderlings, owlken, dream gorgers, and other dark claw-footed denizens with no names. In a journey that was both years and minutes, days, and seconds, he came across the Grove of the Hunter. On a pedestal of bone and sinew was the Horn of the Wild Hunt. A dreadful artifact that would forever alter its player.

    The Prince took the horn with both hands and gave a final farewell to the life he lived. He placed the rough horn to his lips and blew.

    A deep call vibrated across Fairy. All heard the tone in their hearts. All knew what was expected of them. The gentle activities of the Fae were abandoned, as all sought out weapons and took on forms of violence. The Prince's body began a protean shift, his lithe form began to bulk with sinewy ripcord muscle. His hooves that were once as soft as a newborn fawn became as hard as steel. His antlers lost their velvet, and their round points became sharper than a dagger's tip. He was no longer the Prince of Summer's eve, he had become Wildernon, Lord of the Wild Hunt. He reached above him and snapped off a tree's branch that morphed and changed into an antler-headed spear. From the darkest dreams of the woods, Urok, Lord of Stags, walked into the Grove of the Hunter.

"Through the ancient pact, I have come, Wildernon," said Urok.

"Then it is time we hunt," said Wildernon as he mounted the stag before bounding out of the forest. As he road, Wildernon snapped off a point of his antlers and pierced a small wound on the neck of Urok. He took the blood and painted his face, exciting the hunter's instinct. As they rode, others joined them. hawk-riding fae, wielding hunting whips flew next to thorn armed pixies. The heiferkin had become frothing bull-chargers. Dagger-wielding nymphs jumped from tree to tree. Spiderlings coated arrows with deadly venom and poisons. Satyrs broke off branches to use as clubs. All who heard the call took on the wild forms of hunters. Fairy had marshaled quickly, as they charged toward the Reavers.

The War Leader cooed in her babe's ear as she wiped Fae blood from her face. The trails back to their boats were much longer than they had remembered. One of her warriors began to cut designs into trees and found that they were circling back on themselves. As the Reavers discussed what they would do, the Wild Hunt fell upon them. The battle was quick and bloody. The War Leader fought the Fae one-handed as she held her child in her arms. She could do nothing as her warriors were overtaken by the multitude of strange assailants.

"Run, War Leader," shouted her husband. "We will hold them off for as long as we can." The War Leader nodded and took flight into the woods as Wildernon's spear pierced her husband's neck.

The babe cried as she ran through the tangle of the forest. Branches grabbed at her armor and vines clung to her feet as the forest itself sought to hinder her escape. Wildernon was at her heels as he had bounded through the woods as easily as an open field. With raised spear, he threw the weapon, striking the War Leader's leg. With a cry, she collapsed to the earth, shielding her babe from the fall. Wildernon approached her as she pulled her sword out to defend herself.

"Kill me if you must but you will not take my child from me again," she shouted at the towering Lord of the Hunt.

"I am not here to kill you, but to thank you."

"Thank me? I have given you nothing but bloodshed. I expect nothing in return."

"You have given me a most special gift. The gift of rage and hate. You have done what all of Fairy could not. You have cured me of my boredom. For that, you may leave this realm."

The woods behind the War Leader opened to her village. Wildernon pulled his spear from the War Leader's leg causing her to cry out. "Leave my realm and never return. Tell not your kin how you arrived here, or they will meet the point of my spear. Tell your kin to be afraid of the dark corners of the woods for the Wild Hunt has begun, and I do not know when it shall end."

The War Leader, clutching her babe, hobbled away before glancing back in case of treachery. What she found were not the woods of Fairy, but the dark woods of her home and the open arms of her village.

A Gradient into Shadows

New Wave Old Blood

We were drunk on blood and laughter when we left Portland at top speed. Trish took her 1966 black Lincoln Continental out of the garage for this trip. The red leather interior was pristine and soft as coffin velvet. The old radio had been replaced with a state-of-the-art cassette player. This was an apex machine built for cruising American highways. The solitary fault was its seatbelts. I doubt if any vampire had ever used a seatbelt.

Trish and I were siblings tied through vampiric blood, having the same sire. Her idea of a good time was jumping from roof to roof and diving off bridges, while I preferred sneaking into parties I wasn't invited to. We quickly became inseparable and had been getting into trouble ever since.

We left at sunset, and our destination was Los Angeles. The holy city of American performative entertainment. Trish smiled while driving like a hellion, leaving me to coordinate our shoebox of cassette tapes. We agreed that we would only play new music on this trip. No tunes from our mortal days. There would be no ragtime hits or Elvis Presley or anything before 1980.

Bands like *Tears for Fears*, *The Police*, *Duran Duran*, *Depeche Mode*, *The Outfield*, *The Cure*, and *A Flock of Seagulls* were our favorites. We were screaming *Hall & Oates'* "Maneater" as the wind whipped through our hair, and we blitzed down the I-5 toward Los Angeles.

My evening began with the fourth chapter of *Moby Dick*. Then, Trish let herself in through the second-story window of my apartment. She bounced on the couch beside me and draped her arm over my shoulder.

"Hello, my sweet Eileen," she said, licking some blood from her mouth.

"Hi, Trish. You find yourself a snack?" I asked.

"Just a hitchhiker headed for Hollywood," said Trish. "But you are never going to believe what she had on her. Two tickets to the *Duran Duran* show at Santa Monica's beach."

"No way," I said.

"Way," she said as I looked over the tickets.

"Oh, they're for tomorrow night," I said with feigned disappointment.

"Big deal. If we get the Continental, we could be in Los Angeles tomorrow, drinking celebrities' blood and dancing the night away. Sis, Portland has become so boring, and with the elders rejecting my request to sire another vamp, I find myself without any hobbies. I just want to be anyone else besides Trish for a while. A road trip will be perfect. Think about it, in LA you could reinvent yourself into anyone you can imagine. We would fit in perfectly. What's not to love?"

"Desert heat?" I said. "It's murder on my hair."

"That's what hairspray is for. So, what do you think? Want to come along?"

"I don't know, I have so many books I need to read," I

said. I loved the idea of going to Los Angeles. But I needed to play the part of the reluctant older sister. Trish would appreciate it. She loved the idea of being a bad influence on others. Also, I suspected that Trish might find another way to get into trouble if we didn't go on this trip.

"Eileen, I really need to get out of town for a while. If I brought anyone else, they would just lecture me on the duties of the Strigoi. It would be a bummer. You're the only one who knows how to have any fun in this town. Plus, no one should waste their immortality reading *Moby Dick*."

"I don't know, Herman Melville is starting to grow on me," I said.

"Come on, Eileen," she sang.

"Don't you dare!" I said, throwing a pillow at her.

"Come on, Eileen, too loo rye aye!" she sang.

"If you keep singing that song, I will throw you out the window."

"Only if you come with me to LA," she said.

"Alright, it has gotten a bit stuffy in this town. But if we are going to the town of stars, I want to be Joan Jett from her *Bad Reputation* album," I said, closing the book.

"Not *I Love Rock and Roll*?"

"I don't do pink."

"Deal, but I get to be Madonna from her *Borderline* album!"

A pinky promise sealed the deal, and we spent the rest of the evening gathering the supplies. We needed clothing for our personas, hair dye, hair spray, cassettes, sneakers for me, and cute pumps for Trish.

We retrived the Continental and found a truck stop that allowed us to put our costumes on. I dyed my hair black while Trish bleached out her current hair, leaving plenty of dark roots to get Madonna's glamorous look. It wasn't long before we roared onto the interstate with *Duran Duran's* "Rio" at the highest volume the car could muster.

We tore through Oregon like we had robbed a bank. We were stopped twice for speeding, but a bit of charm and hypnosis forced the cops to tear up our tickets.

Northern California's treacherous winding roads proved no trouble for Trish as she hurtled around the tight curves.

The all-consuming darkness that made driving dangerous for a mortal was nothing to her. We had gone through most of our cassettes, and we most certainly would be listening to them on repeat for the foreseeable future.

"Hey, Trish, why do vampires make terrible chiropractors?" I asked.

"I don't know, why?"

"They're a pain in the neck," I said.

"That's terrible. Why did the vampire get married?"

"It was love at first bite?"

"Yep. Oh, I got another one!" she said. "What do baby vampires and lollipops have in common?"

"They're both little suckers."

"How are you so good at those?" asked Trish.

"Lots of practice," I said. "I have been trying to get an elder to laugh for ages. Heck, I'd take a smile."

"It's because that's one of their rules," she said, taking a tone of mock seriousness. "Don't tell the mortals of your nature. The number of Strigoi shall remain fixed. Break any of these rules and we will kill you and your entire bloodline. And of course, never smile."

"They take that last one very seriously," I said.

"They take them all too seriously; I mean, come on, break one rule, and it's an automatic death sentence? It's not fair," said Trish.

"Well, I have been around long enough to know that fair or not, they are very practical rules to keep us safe. There are so many more humans than us that if we were discovered, it would be the end of all of us. That's why we gotta keep our numbers in check."

"Yeah, I guess," she said. "Hey, do you ever wonder what it would be like if we were still mortal?"

"Where did that come from?" I said.

"I don't know. Just a thought."

"We would be little old ladies," I said, making my best geriatric impression. "We would be surrounded by drooling grandchildren by now, and I would probably have great-grandchildren running around, and we wouldn't be making any sort of trips except to the hospital or funeral home. A bullet dodged, if you ask me."

"You make that sound like having a family is the dullest thing in the world," said Trish.

"I once had dreams of having a family. Glad I got over that idea. I would much rather see what the next few centuries will bring. I mean, when I was turned in 1909, we were still in horse-drawn carriages, and in just sixty years, we landed a man on the moon. Who knows what the future will bring?"

"Shit! Is that daylight? We are going to have to switch," she said, pulling off to the side of the road. "I wish I could drive in the daylight. I don't know how you tolerate it."

"That's what sunglasses are for."

Bram Stoker got it right. While I like early 20th-century German films as much as the next gal, *Nosferatu* was a little off when it came to burning up in the sunlight. We do have trouble in the daylight. We're sluggish, and our charms and trances aren't as effective. Sunlight is usually too much for a freshly turned vamp. From my own experience, it took me years before I could even walk in the daylight.

I closed the top of the Continental, and we turned the air conditioner as low as it would go. The journey the rest of the day was dull. Neither of us had any pep in the daylight. All chatter was relegated to checking the map and pointing out license plates from different states.

Our music, while constant, wasn't as loud as we drifted through Yuba City, Sacramento, Stockton, past Bakersfield, and finally made it to Los Angeles at twilight.

We had no plan when we arrived in Los Angeles. Half the fun was riding the twists and turns of fate. The lethargy we felt began to vanish as the sun dipped below the horizon. Our listless muscles became whipcord tight. Trish had put the Continental's top-down so we could feel the rush of wind.

"We should go to the beach so we can get a good view of the stage," she shouted.

"We will, but we can't go straight there. We've got to pace ourselves. See the sights, build up the moments before releasing them in a sublime apotheosis," I said, applying a fresh coat of lipstick.

"What the hell are you talking about?" she said, taking her turn with the lipstick.

"I'm talking about emotional catharsis. Do you fire off

the biggest firework first on the fourth of July? No, you shoot off a bunch of little ones and then end with a bang."

"So, the show is the big firework? Since when? I thought this was *my* trip?"

"This is *our* trip," I said. "*Duran Duran* isn't going anywhere. Now, throw on some Billy Idol; we sang "Rebel Yell" as we took a right at Sun Valley into North Hollywood.

"Then where do we go if the beach is some sort of emotional orgasm?" asked Trish.

"Don't say it like that, but I think the Hollywood Walk of Fame would be a good start."

"God, you are such a tourist and a prude to boot." She laughed. I didn't.

"Take it back," I said, my pupils constricting to pinholes, the corners of my mouth curling to a fanged snarl.

"What?" said Trish, realizing too late that my blood was boiling in a frenzy. "Oh god! Sorry. I take it back, you're not a tourist, or a prude, or whatever!"

"That's what I thought," I said, returning to the road. Trish remained pressed against the door of the Continental.

She was ready to jump out of the car onto the freeway if necessary. I took deep, controlled breaths. I was ready to bite and tear Trish apart. A few minutes passed without a word spoken as I collected myself. Billy Idol's "Rebel Yell" drifted into *Toto*'s "Hold the Line."

"I'm sorry, Trish, I didn't mean to pull the fangs out."

"Hey, no big thing, girlfriend. We'll move past it, and go see some stars," she said.

"So...what was it that got the fangs out?"

"You called me a prude."

"I don't understand."

"When I was mortal, if you weren't into petting, you were a prude. In the crowd I ran with that meant being cut from the herd. All the friends I had made over the years just abandoned me. I'm not a prude, and I don't want that to be the excuse for people to write me off."

"There is nothing wrong with being a little old-fashioned," said Trish. She had been practicing her maternal voice. She needed to work on it.

"I know that. I'm not the same woman I was from so

long ago. But I still want sex to be with someone special. I want it to mean something."

"That makes sense. That's kind of romantic, in a way," said Trish. "God, I forget how different our mortal lives were sometimes. When I was mortal, I was such a flirt. It was something we were all doing back then."

"I remember the fifties being a buttoned-up time."

"It was only skin deep; duck and cover got all of us rattled. Why do you think there were so many babies during that time?" She chuckled. "Hey! At least you aren't like one of those snooty Victorians who thinks a letter and holding hands was first base."

"Small mercies," I said, turning up the stereo as *Tears for Fears'* "Everybody Wants to Rule the World" roared from the speakers.

When we made it to the Walk of Fame, I tranced some tourists and stole their parking space. Trancing was a trick I was good at, but Trish had no talent for it. She made up for it by having a dancer's grace and a bodybuilder's strength.

By now, the sun was casting incandescent light on the

clouds. Looking down, we saw the stars of almost a century's worth of actors below our feet. Most other civilizations made great statues of conquerors, killers, and kings. Some of them turned their philosophers and poets into stone monuments. Only America would immortalize the star. Someone who was pretending to be anybody else.

"I found Brando!" shouted Trish.

"Who?"

"Marlon Brando!" she said, dropping her voice in imitation. "'You don't understand. I could have had class, I could have been a contender, I could have been somebody, instead of a bum!' From *On the Waterfront*."

"Oh yeah! I haven't seen that film in years!"

"We should rent it from the video store when we get back to Portland. Who have you found?" she asked.

"I found Lauren Bacall, Buster Keaton, and Groucho Marx."

"I don't know who any of those people are, except Groucho. I didn't peg you for the talk show type," said Trish as we continued walking.

"I never saw his talk show. I just remember seeing him in vaudeville. You can't imagine my surprise when I saw him and his brothers on the big screen."

"He was in movies?" said Trish. "We will have to add it to the watch list."

We kept moving past the mortals who watched the living statues, the magicians, and the actor impersonators. We stopped so Trish could squeal over Marilyn Monroe's star. A bouquet of red roses was placed on her square with a card that read "In loving memory."

"I can't believe it has been over twenty years since she passed," whispered Trish. "How do you deal with it?"

"Deal with what?" I asked as Trish crouched down to the star and traced Monroe's name with her finger.

"You know, the passing of years, watching the mortals bloom and turn to dust, while we remain like Polaroid pictures," asked Trish. Trish had a strange quiver in her voice. This sadness came bursting forth from some hidden place that she kept concealed. I caught glimpses of it on rainy days and around winter nights approaching Christmas. I crouched down and put my hand on her shoulder. I would need to play the wise sister to get Trish through this.

"I don't know. I try not to think about their lives too much. I don't know if any of us really wants to think about it for too long. I'm just as new to this as you. Maybe ask me again in a hundred years. Come on, I need to hunt. Driving in the sun wipes a girl out."

"Yeah, it does," said Trish as she stood up. The gloom between us had vanished. I was content to get moving, but Trish saw something.

"A baby!" squealed Trish as she ran over to a young couple with a stroller. I was not far behind. We grinned like idiots as we crouched down around the little human. It was wrapped up in a floral pattern blanket with a powder blue hat on its head.

"How old is it," I asked.

"She is three months old," said the mother.

"What's her name?" asked Trish.

"Her name is Mary. After the mother of Christ," said the father. "You girls sure are excited." The pair seemed amused by our attention. They smiled at each other as they watched us.

"Sorry, we get excited by new things," I said. Trish and I almost screamed when the baby woke up.

"Oh my god, Eileen, she's waking up!" whispered Trish. The baby shifted in her stroller, yawned, and opened her eyes to find two apex predators leering at her. The fear came on quickly for baby Mary. I don't know if it was the fangs, the big hair, or our intense gaze, but baby Mary began to cry. This always happened when we got too close to babies.

"Aww poor girl's upset," said the father.

"I'm so sorry," shouted Trish.

"It's alright girls, she is just a little moody from being out so late," said the mother, leaning down while adjusting the blanket. "You girls have a good evening."

"Come on, Trish," I said, pulling her with me.

"Oh my god, she was so cute, I just wanted to kiss her for days," smiled Trish.

"I know, right on her little button nose."

"Hey, we should get a hotel before the show starts," said Trish. "I think we should find one near the beach. I feel I am nearing that...what was it you called it?"

"Sublime apotheosis?"

"Yeah, if I don't get that white sand between my toes tonight, I might just explode."

"Alright. Race you to the car!" I said, taking off at the speed of an Olympic sprinter.

"Oh, you're on," shouted Trish as she took off her high heels and gave chase. I thought I could beat her with a head start, but I was no match for Trish's raw athleticism. She quickly passed me as we ran almost the entire length of the mile in about five minutes. We hopped into the car and drove onto the streets of Los Angeles.

Finding a hotel within walking distance of the beach was easy enough. I was itching to feed, but Trish insisted on attending the show early.

"Come on. Let's find some hunky beach bums. There will be plenty of people to choose from, and no one will notice if one or two people go missing during the show," she said, tugging me past the hotel bar. I was eyeing the mortals inside. The bar was my kind of hunting ground. Even without the trance, I can always find someone to take away into the night. I barely saw the people anymore, just the veins and arteries running along their necks and arms. But eating some prime rib bodybuilder instead of the skinny bar fare was persuasive.

"Let's go," I said. I wanted to hunt. I wanted to feel hot blood in my mouth. Trish was feeling it as well. An urge that could only be held off for so long. Like holding your breath underwater. Eventually, you must come up for air.

We said little as we made our way to the beach. I was excited. There are few things as thrilling to an immortal as the hunt. Some of the elders would spend months tracking a single person. They would learn their subtle patterns and find the perfect time to strike. Right now, I wasn't not so patient. We didn't need the car as we went to Santa Monica's Beach. Trish had to take off her pumps while walking on the sand. I followed suit just to feel the sand under my feet. In the distance, we could see that the show had already started with a local warm-up act. A sizeable crowd of mortals could be seen a mile off.

"The moon's out," shouted Trish.

"Too bad it's not a full moon. That would have made

this perfect," I replied, breathing the briny ocean air.

"I wouldn't have it any other way." She smiled. "It's perfect."

"Did you reach your apotheosis?" I asked, scanning the beach for potential prey.

"Not yet, but I know I will find it tonight." The moon was so bright that it cast its luminous glow on the waves. Starlight on the black void of the deep. It was distracting enough that I didn't notice the other vampires approaching us. There were four of them, all swim trunks and tank tops, with baseball caps and sandals that covered weather-beaten limbs. Their leader was a boy in his early twenties, but we couldn't tell his true age without tasting his blood.

"Time to turn around," he said. "Locals only. That goes double for vampires."

"You've got to be joking," I said. "We came down to see the show, and last time I checked, this was a free country."

"And you are free to explore the whole width and breadth of it. But this beach is for locals, I don't care if some dust-in-the-wind mortal is having a show or not," the leader replied. I wanted to tear this guy up and throw him in the ocean. I was confident in Trish's ability to kick ass, and I had danced with a rival vampire or two in my time. But there were so many unknowns involved here.

"Let's go somewhere else, Eileen," she said, taking me by the arm and pulling me back.

"What? We aren't going to listen to these jerks, are we?"

"Eileen, it's not worth it; I don't have to be in the crowd to enjoy the show."

"Glad you understand our position."

"Whatever, asshole," said Trish, pulling me toward the Santa Monica pier. I gave them the finger before turning on my heel. The pier was lit up like Christmas. The Ferris wheel spun like a firecracker with reds, blues, and purples.

"Hey! Let's go to the pier. We should find someone to eat there. Plus, we can get a good view of the show."

"No, I was thinking we should split up for a bit," she said, looking out at the Pacific. "There is something I need to do, and you obviously need to hunt alone for a bit. Get the built-up aggression out."

"Trish, did I do something wrong?"

"It's not you, really," she said before turning to me. "I want to go and get something I've wanted for a very long time."

"What is it?"

"You will see when you get back at the hotel. You go hunt and stay away from those locals," she said.

"Yeah, sure thing."

"Alright, see you back at the hotel!" She winked.

"I'll see you then," I replied. A moment later, Trish turned into mist and was sailing away. I put my sneakers back on. I was on the hunt.

I walked onto the pier. The place was bursting with mortal life. A young man with a radio was playing *Journey*'s "Separate Ways." I was invisible in the mass of humanity. Just another soul amongst thousands. I was looking for a loner; targeting a couple or clique would draw too much attention. Then I found her. A crying young woman was leaning on the railing, looking at the ocean.

"Everything alright?" I asked.

"It's nothing," she said, wiping her eyes.

"Doesn't seem like it," I replied. "Come on. Tell a perfect stranger your problem."

"It's silly," she said, putting her head in her hands. "But I didn't get the part for the movie I auditioned for. I'm such an idiot to ever think I would ever make it."

"It's just a setback," I replied. "With looks like yours, you're going to be a star in no time."

"That's nice of you to say," she said, scooting closer to me. "But I'm a terrible actress, it just took that audition for me to finally realize it. Now I'm just another nobody."

"That's not true. You're you, and you're one of a kind," I said.

"If only that could pay my rent. I'm so stupid. I really thought putting on a costume and some makeup would turn me into a great actress."

"You know, the costume is only half the battle," I said, moving almost close enough to touch as we leaned on the rails.

"Oh really?"

"I'm serious, I have been in the acting business a very long time."

"Oh yeah? Then why haven't I ever seen you before?"

"I mostly do street-level work."

"Is that why you're dressed as Joan Jett?" she asked. Her cheeks were so rosy, so full of blood.

"A little bit. But I have played lots of other roles. The diligent student, frightened victim, devoted fiancée, mourning widow, a woman out of time, best friend, caring sister. My favorite roles are the femme fatales."

"Why that one?"

"Because a femme fatale is both mysterious and dangerous, always keeping the audience guessing."

"I wish I had your confidence." She smiled, looking back to the sea. "Maybe I wasn't cut out for this acting thing."

"You want to hear an acting secret?" I asked, leaning forward. She nodded, her eyes lighting up. I leaned close to her ear.

"The trick is to find a mask that fits, and then never take it off."

I then bit her neck. She went limp. I grabbed her and threw us both into the surf. Our splash went unnoticed by the mass of humanity above. Under the waves, I was free to feed in peace. The life in her body slowly vanished. When she was dead, I licked the wound on her neck closed, and with a fingernail as sharp as any razor, I cut open her wrists. Then, all I had to do was let the ocean take her away. If anyone found her, they would just assume she was just another tragic suicide.

I spent an hour walking around town. Trish had asked how I dealt with the mortal world turning to dust. It's easy when you must end mortal life so frequently. Immortality had its price. But the feeling after a kill is like nothing else. A vampire is flush and alive. It's a feeling of euphoria and exhaustion that can only be achieved through the best type of sex or the most damaging of drugs. It takes time to get over that rush. The stolen life made the world sharp and vivid. It made smells more acute, and coarse cotton feel like velvet.

I found a club and danced till my legs turned to jelly. Until the rush of the blood wore off, and I was once again stuck in my thoughts. The blood high made me completely forget about Trish. I suspected she had enough time to do what she needed to. So, I returned to the hotel. However, when I got back, I regretted taking so long.

I found Trish in the hotel with a young man in her lap. His neck had been savaged. Trish's mouth and neck were covered in blood. She was stroking his hair while he breathed raggedly.

"What did you do?" I said, locking the door.

"I'm sorry, Eileen. I had to. But it's OK! His name is James," she said, stroking his hair. James's eyes were wild, his mind and body still reeling from the painful conversion from life to living death.

"You sired him! Let me see your wrists!" I said, grabbing her arms. As I suspected, her wrists were cut to allow her blood to flow into James's dying body. "Shit, I leave you alone for a couple of hours and you go and sire a mortal."

"Don't talk to me like I'm a *child!* I would be a grandmother now if I was still alive," she said, ripping her hand out of my grip. "I have been waiting decades for this chance and I took it."

"Shit," I said, pacing back and forth. "What the hell are we going to do?"

"Don't worry. We are going to take James back to Portland and teach him all he needs to know," she said, kissing his forehead.

"Are you kidding me? Trish, there are rules, there are a fixed number of vampires. You would have been able to turn a mortal in time. All you had to do was wait for some idiot tick to get dusted."

"In what, a hundred years? I am the youngest vampire in Portland. There are dozens of vampires ahead of me. It could be centuries before I get a chance like this again. We can just pass him off as a friend we found."

"That's not going to work. This James won't know anything, he will be caught and put to death. Just like you will be when they find out you turned him." I was on the verge of shouting. "Trish, I can't lose you. You are my blood sister, my only friend. Everyone else I ever knew is either in a nursing home or a cemetery. I can't lose another friend. I can't lie about this, and I can't let you jeopardize your eternity. It's too risky."

Trish stumbled, leaving James on the bed. "Then what do you expect me to do. When I was alive, I had one thing on my mind and that was motherhood. It's kind of hard to do that now that I'm sterile. I will never be a real mother. Siring is the closest thing I will have to a family!"

"You have a family," I whispered. "We are a family."

"I don't know if that is enough. I'm afraid it might be too late for me."

"Trish, I can understand you are going through a tough spot. I can help you get out of it. But that means letting this man go."

"No! You can't take this from me. James is mine, my child."

"Trish, I'm not trying to steal from you; I'm trying to rescue you. You are the only one I can be real with. That's what ties us together."

"It was just a coincidence; we were just the youngest in a town of geriatric leeches," she said, gripping my hand so tightly it hurt.

"That still doesn't change the fact that I can't lose you.

If we go back to Portland with James, you both will be killed. If you stay, you will be killed by the locals. I can save you Trish, but only you."

"What do we have to do?" she asked, tears of blood rolling down her face.

"I think you know," I whispered.

Trish shook her head in protest. "I can't."

"Yes, you can, you have the strength to do it." She closed her eyes and looked away. "Listen, I will keep James' attention and hold him in place. Alright?" She gritted her teeth. Her fangs bared as the blood ran across her cheeks. "OK, I'll get him ready."

I pulled James off the bed onto his feet. Positioning him beside the bed and letting gravity bring him to his knees was a simple affair.

"What is going on?" he asked, licking his lips.

"Just look into my eyes," I replied, trancing him. "Think of the happiest moment of your life."

He smiled with his eyes glazed over. Trish moved behind him. I nodded. She shook her head. "Trish, I'm not as strong as you, this is our only option." Bloody tears dripped off her chin when she placed her hands below his jaw.

"I'm sorry," she whispered before using all her might to rip James' head from his body. He was reduced to ash, and his empty clothes fell into a grey pile. Trish collapsed and began to cry on my shoulder. I held her tight, fearing that if I let her go, I would lose her forever.

A Gradient into Shadows

The Black Mountain Hearing

Allen stared out the window to the D.C. street, where a protest was underway. The sun bathed the protestors with a thin yellow light that was all wrong. He idly sparked the flint on his lighter, sending out an occasional flame that had no heat and was cold as ice. He compulsively lit the lighter, feeling the icy flame on his finger. Things were happening faster than he had expected, and nobody had noticed. He turned back to the senators, who were ready for their hearing.

There were three senators of importance in this meeting: Senator Johnathan Baldwin, Senator Amanda Corwick, and Senator Gabriel Torres. The six other senators would stay quiet and follow their lead. Eleven people were crammed into this tiny room, including the stenographer.

"Please state your name for the record," said Senator Corwick.

"My full name is Allen Michal Joffre."

"And what is your occupation?" asked Corwick.

"I was a guard at the Black Mountain facility run by an arm of the pentagon, specifically working on Operation Watchtower."

"Mr. Joffre," began Senator Baldwin, "there are several things peculiar about this meeting, namely, that on the one hand just finding you has been an exercise in bureaucratic lunacy. Just getting you in that seat has taken over a thousand hours of investigation, and interagency negotiations. You have a PhD in economics, and a Master's in ethics, and contemporary armed conflict. For goodness' sake, you have a higher security clearance than the vice president. I find it hard to believe that you are just a guard at the Black Mountain facility."

"Well, that was what my job essentially was," replied Allen, "I was a guard at that facility. The same way a triggerman at a nuclear missile silo guards the country."

"Mr. Joffre," interjected Torres, "I fail to see how you and those that can unleash nuclear Armageddon have anything in common."

"We are getting ahead of ourselves," said Corwick. "Today's inquiry is how a multibillion-dollar installation was destroyed. An installation so secret, not even the president of the United States knew its location."

"I'm just determining how Mr. Joffre fits into all this," said Baldwin.

"Shall I take it from the top?" asked Allen. "I think that will explain a thing or two."

"Please do," replied Corwick.

"Well, before we can talk about the installation and my place in it, we need to talk about Nineveh."

"Nineveh? What the heck is that?" asked Senator Baldwin.

"It's a city, John," said Torres.

"Now how in God's name do you know that, Gabe?" asked Baldwin.

"It's in the Bible, John. If I remember right, it is the ancient Assyrian capital."

"That's correct, senator, located near the modern-day city of Mosul in Iraq."

"So, what does it have to do with our destroyed installation," asked Baldwin.

"Well, sir, it provides context to my mission at Black Mountain. You see an artifact was dug out of the ruins of the city's palace. A British expedition in 1913 was on a dig when the leader of the expedition, Sir Walter Hastings, found a hidden chamber, a chamber that contained the mirror."

"While fascinating, I am skeptical of the relevance to this hearing," said Torres.

"It is very much relevant. You see, Sir Walter had no idea what he had found. The mirror is at the heart of Operation Watchtower. It is the sole reason that the Black Mountain installation was destroyed in the first place," said Allen.

"Now this mirror isn't some sort of codename, is it?" asked Torres.

"No, it's literal. But it's not quite a mirror, even if it

appears to be. It's configured like a vanity table, like something my ex-wife would have sat at to do her makeup. The thing is made of polished stained wood, with a singular red button in the center."

"Excuse me?" replied Baldwin. "Last time I checked. Wood tends to fall apart after a certain length of time. I have seen wood rot to pieces over a summer. There is no way it could have lasted from biblical times."

"Well, this was no ordinary artifact. Its durability was the least curious thing about it."

"Please continue," replied Corwick.

"Well, the First World War broke out before Walter could take it to a British museum. He promptly went home and was killed in the battle of the Somme. Flash forward twenty years later, the Nazis are doing their whole Aryan genealogy thing in the near east, and a Nazi S.S. officer by the name of… oh what was it, oh yes, Otis Stotch. Old Otis finds the mirror, puts it with the other artifacts he looted, and forgets about it. Well, until he got back to Germany, stark raving mad. He was committed and was then liquidated by the Reich. Fast forward to the end of the war, and Operation Paperclip is in full swing. You know the operation where we tried to get as many Nazi scientists as we could before the Soviets snatched them up?"

"The panel is aware of Operation Paperclip. I take it that this is how the U.S. government came into possession of this mirror?" said Corwick.

"Yes, senator. It came with Dr. Luthor Petersohn, later changed to Peterson to make it more Anglo. Dr. Peterson is the one responsible for laying the foundations for Operation Watchtower," said Allen.

"And just what is Operation Watchtower?" asked Baldwin.

"Well, for that we have to get into game theory, and Cold War modes of thinking."

"Explain," said Corwick.

"Well, in short, game theory is a mathematical and logical approach in deciding how to act in uncertain outcomes. For instance, how do you win a nuclear war? Well, you can strike first and trigger retaliation that kills both players. Neither players wants to die, so you have a stalemate. But the thing is, both players want things, so the game is finding ways of getting things from your opponent without triggering Armageddon. Game theory was built on that model to find an optimal outcome without our destruction."

"So, Project Watchtower is a nuclear deterrent?" asked Torres.

"Kind of," said Allen, "But it is not a nuclear threat we were worried about. No, what we were concerned with was an extra-dimensional threat."

The room erupted in muttering. Allen took the time to sip his water. The liquid tasted sour. Things were changing too quickly. He looked out the window and saw that it was snowing. It was July.

"Extra-dimensional?" asked Torres, "Is this some kind of joke?"

"No. I never was much of a comedian."

"Well, it sounds particularly ridiculous to me," said Baldwin.

"Gentlemen," interjected Corwick, "Need I remind you how much time and taxpayer money it took to get Mr. Joffre sitting here today. Now please continue, what was the nature of this so-called extra-dimensional threat?"

"Well, senator, the mirror was a view to another dimension, much like our own. The button I mentioned would destroy the opposite dimension in five seconds," said Allen.

"I would like to point out that this is increasingly sounding insane," said Baldwin. "From where I sit, two scenarios exist. One is that Mr. Joffre is delusional and should seek immediate psychiatric help, or two, the U.S. government had a rogue department, with no supervision, with access to billions of taxpayers' money. Considering Mr. Joffre's security clearance, I don't know which is more horrifying."

"This is not at all surprising, John, the Pentagon is a black hole of bureaucracy and byzantine spending practices," said Torres.

"Gabe, this is not a time for your soapbox," said Baldwin.

"Gentlemen, we will stick to the topic at hand," said Corwick. "Now Mr. Joffre, when, if ever, have you had a psychological evaluation."

"Under the program, I was required to have a weekly psychological evaluation, as the active stress is very similar to what you might find from someone operating the trigger mechanism of a nuclear missile."

"I see," said Corwick. "So, in theory, pressing this button would destroy the other universe, and Project Watchtower existed to keep this mirror from falling into unscrupulous hands."

"Not entirely true, senator. "You see the other dimension has a similar button on their side of the mirror," said Allen. The room grew quiet.

"So, your position at the Black Mountain facility was to guard this mirror?" asked Torres.

"No, I was to press the button in the event the other dimension chose to press their own."

"So, in this hypothetical arrangement, you worked under a scenario of mutually assured destruction?" asked Baldwin.

"Yes, senator."

"Mr. Joffre is there any proof of this mirror's existence,

any proof that verifies your claim?" asked Torres.

"The proof is buried under a literal mountain of rubble," replied Allen.

"About that," said Baldwin. "While this fantasy you have constructed may be amusing, it does not explain how the mountain was destroyed in the first place."

"Well, senator, we had to initiate the facility's self-destruction protocols. That mountain was honeycombed with enough explosives to level a major metropolitan city ten times over. It was a safeguard in case any foreign agents or domestic entities tried to take control of it. We couldn't run the risk of a non-Watchtower entity taking the mirror. Doing so would give the other side a slim opportunity to destroy our universe."

"So how did this last resort protocol get triggered?" asked Torres.

"Well, for that, you will need to first learn about the other side and my opposite number, Siddomner. I called him Sid. Anyway, Sid and I had been staring at each other down for about three years now. Standard procedure for both sides of the mirror involved having a second nearby in the event the primary guard were to have a health failure or spontaneously commits suicide."

"What do you mean spontaneously?" asked Baldwin.

"Hazards of the job. My predecessor snuck in a razor blade and sliced himself to ribbons right in front of Sid. It was a near-miss event. Thankfully, I persuaded Sid to keep his hands off that button. Anyway, Sid comes from a society unlike our own. It developed along a much different socio-political path. Sid was human, but his universe had different pressures on it, thus creating very different people. From what I can tell, Sid came from a regimented, horizontally hierarchical clan-based system of government, which in turn was part of a tight coalition of peoples. They had no notions of nation-states. They had an industrial revolution but still used swords and armor. By necessity, we had learned and become fluent in each other's language. I can count on one hand how many people can speak Sid's language fluently. Anyway, Sid was a nice enough guy; he always made sure that the painted picture of his family could be seen from my side. Just to make me a little less likely to press that button. He wrote poetry and loved chess; one of the crazy things was that the other side also thought of chess. But they had different names for the pieces.

"The guy was the very model of stoicism. Liked to put on a brave face, right up to the very end." Allen hadn't realized he was choking up. He stopped and collected himself.

"Take your time, Mr. Joffre," said Corwick. Allen took a deep breath and took a sip of water. It now tasted like the electric tang of a 9-volt battery.

"Anyway, I was the point man on the day we initiated the facility self-destruct system, I was to relieve another button jockey. A crisis was unfolding when I got into that damn room. The other point man, who I will call Wilson, as his name has not been cleared for…you know what it doesn't matter, his name was Tom."

"Are we cleared to even hear that?" asked Torres.

"As I said, it doesn't matter. Whatever secret laws and regulations I have broken just by sitting here are irrelevant at this point. You see, the other side of the mirror was going through a crisis. If only that bastard Tom only pushed that damn button." Allen pulled out a pack of cigarettes and lit it.

The ice-cold flame lit the cigarette, sending cold air into his mouth.

"Mr. Joffre, you cannot smoke in here," said Corwick.

"Senator, if you want to hear how this story unfolds you have to indulge me."

"Oh, let him have it, Amanda, this whole hearing is a farce anyway," said Baldwin, "Any chance I can get one of those?"

"Johnathan!" said Corwick.

"People, we are getting off track," said Torres.

"I agree," sighed Corwick. "Because of the particular nature of this meeting, I will allow it, but be advised you may suffer fines from the city; Mr. Joffre, please continue."

"Alright, senator. You see, when I came in, Tom informed me of the crises that were unfolding in the other world. He was passing that hot potato right into my lap because he wasn't man enough to do what needed to be done. I don't think I was either, but what was done was done. When I checked in on Sid, I found that he hadn't been sleeping and alarms were going off. He was begging me to press the button."

"Really?" asked Torres.

"Yes, senator, Sid was begging me to destroy his universe. Now, due to the nature of the mirror, all communication had to be done in writing, as sound could not travel through the mirror. So, I slap a note on the mirror. 'What is going on?' I ask. I get a 'no time to explain' back.

"You see, Sid is an interesting guy; he was ready to press his button at the drop of the hat. If you moved too fast or whatever, he would already be in the position to press the button. Sid knew the risks and dangers of threatening to wipe out another universe. He was no dummy. More than anything, he wanted to keep his family safe. So, when he starts begging me to murder his universe, I get concerned.

"So, I ask, 'Sid I'm going to need more than that, I'm not going to destroy billions of people or snuff out a trillion galaxies of another universe without good cause, my conscience won't allow it. Self-defense is one thing, but our two universes have been engaging in a tolerable co-existence since the program began. I mean, imagine if someone from one of our geopolitical rivals started begging us to wipe out their country, burn it to rubble, and salt the earth. No model of game theory could account for that move. Playing to win is one thing, and playing not to lose is how the game is played, but playing to lose is such an anathema to the model that I...I'm getting sidetracked. Long and short of it, I was in the dark on how to play the hand I was dealt."

"So, what was happening on the other side of the mirror?" asked Torres.

"Well, Sid informs me that they had another mirror to another dimension, well technically they had three. One for us and two others. Two different coalitions of clans held the other two, and each of the three major coalition blocks was responsible for their mirror. Sid tells me that something had broken through one of the mirrors."

"Excuse me?" said Baldwin.

"Yes, something broke through one of the other mirrors. Sid used the word *god* or *demon*. Whatever it was, it was big, and it was devouring whole ecosystems. Their clans had been battling it for about a week before we were ever aware of it. By then, Sid's universe was going through a massive extinction event; the thing from the other mirror was devouring all life and disrupting the very fabric of reality. Basic things like thermodynamics were falling apart, cause happened before effect. Sid said that the entity was devouring the universe. What's worse was that it had already gotten to their third mirror and broken through that one."

"I'm sorry this is ridiculous," interjected Baldwin, "This whole story is a fabricated delusion. Dimension devouring entities? Cold war-style communication mirrors? If this isn't psychosis, then it's a farce and a waste of this hearing's time."

"It's all true, senator, I was there, and in about, oh, three weeks' time, our reality will be consumed by that very same monster."

"What do you mean?" asked Corwick.

"It all comes down to the conclusion of our story. You see, the entity was searching for these mirrors so it could destroy other dimensions. Now, Sid could have very easily destroyed our reality and deprived the monster of food. We would naturally destroy his universe in retaliation; after all, the threat doesn't work if there is no fist to back it up. But you see, Sid's worldview comes into play. He believed that at the very least someone should survive. If his reality is doomed, then it might as well be destroyed so it could be cut off from our own. I didn't have a lot of time to make a good decision as the entity had already started crashing through Sid's doorway. He tells me to press the button, before drawing his sword and charging the entity."

"And what, pray tell, did this entity look like?" asked Torres. Allen had to stop and think; memories flashed in his mind, and his mouth dried up. The water in his glass was bubbling.

"So, you know how in old televisions there used to be that black and white static between channels? The entity looked like that, but it was formed like a giant octopus the size of a blue whale. Well, old Sid charged the thing, God preserve him, and the thing unmade him."

"Unmade? You mean killed?" asked Baldwin.

"No, unmade. From what I could tell, the entity stripped him of each of his elements, one at a time, reducing him to a pulsing pile of dust and sludge. That's when I pressed the button. I can't say it was a conscious act, just an automatic reaction from years of training, like how cops or soldiers are trained to shoot anyone who charges them. They just do it on muscle memory. I pressed the button right as the entity slammed into the glass. The glass cracked and splintered, and you have to keep in mind that the Watchtower scientists used diamond drill bits on that mirror surface and didn't make a scratch. But this thing was cracking it. That's when the mirror went dark. The other universe vanished, leaving a dark void in its place." Allen sighed before leaning back in the uncomfortable chair. "End of story, right? Well, there is still the matter of how the facility was destroyed."

"Right now, that crater that was once a mountain is the only piece of verifiable fact in your story, so yes, an explanation would be appreciated," said Corwick.

"A piece of the entity got through. A small piece no bigger than a pen immediately started causing havoc. Tom, the dumb bastard, thought it would be a good idea to stomp on it. For the second time in as many minutes, I saw someone unmade.

"We used everything to try and kill that thing. We shot that stupid worm only to have our bullets wind up in the shooter's brains. We think it was bending space around it. Fire did nothing to it, neither did acid or electricity. We spent half a day trying to destroy this tiny piece of the entity, to no effect. Worse yet, it was growing. After a day of trying to contain it, it was the size of a large dog. That's when we decided to destroy the facility. To bury it so deep that it would give us time to do what we needed to do."

"And what might that be?" asked Baldwin.

"To get the word out, you see, if Sid's universe has three mirrors, then maybe ours does as well. If we can find the mirrors, then maybe we could get them to press their button." The whole room erupted in whispered muttering and shocked disbelief.

"If what you are saying is true, and I by no means think it is, you want us to commit universal suicide?" asked Torres.

"Yes, the heads of Project Watchtower do not think the entity could be stopped in any conceivable manner besides cutting it off from its food supply. It all comes back to game theory. The core belief of nuclear conflict is not to be destroyed. That is the singular win condition, not defeating the opponent but staying alive. You see, we thought we were engaging in a confrontational game; instead, we were part of a cooperative one.

"Now I ask you this, is it more ethical to have both players killed if someone pulls the trigger? Or is it more ethical to let one player die so the other player survives? Our existence will inevitably lead to the death of other players in the game. So, we must give the other players on the board a chance to live, because right now, something is eating the pieces."

There was silence in the room; no one spoke. A loud cough from one of the minor senators sent cold reverberations through the room.

"I think we are at a good stopping point today," said Corwick. "Are there any final comments you would like to make?"

"Yes, there is," replied Allen, inhaling the last of his cigarette before dropping the butt in the water. The cup caught fire, sending off steaming smoke that turned to icicles on the ceiling. "I don't intend to be seeing this through, I don't want to be seeing anyone unmade again, so like my predecessor, I snuck in a razor blade."

A Gradient into Shadows

The Coiling Dark

Kenny was on the road to Alturas California, traveling from the rippling lightshow that was Reno. The gaudy yellow and red lights that had cast Reno in a dim ember glow, were now gone. Now there was only the winding dark of the road. The night sky was moonless or overcast. Kenny couldn't tell which. All he knew was that the night closed in on him, his weak headlights barely combating the all-consuming dark. In this ink he finally understood what it was like to be a deep-sea fish, swimming through the oppressive night. Occasionally, the darkness was split by the headlights of a passing car, surprising him from around one of the many winding bends of California's roads. His eyes locked onto those blobs of light, trapping his vision in the luminous glow. His sight was briefly overwhelmed before leaving him once again with his weak headlights in the crushing dark.

In his hand, Kenny rubbed the eleven-month AA chip. The chip was bright red in daylight, but in the dark it was reduced to tactile sensation. With his thumb he could make out the triangle of its surface easily enough, as well as the circled eleven. Kenny could only guess what the inscription was with his thumb, thankfully he had his memory as his guide.

"To thine own self be true. Unity, service, Recovery, Month," these words gave him inspiration these last eleven mouths. He guessed the text with his thumb, a silly game to pass the time as he blitzed through the night at seventy miles an hour. Five miles above the speed limit.

Technically illegal. But it was the type of pernicious behavior that society expected. He knew he would be in trouble if he was stopped for something else. However, in the vast distance between towns in this primeval desert and squat mountains, he doubted there would be any police within two hundred miles. So, he broke the law at an acceptable speed and fought boredom the best he could as he made his way home. He wished his wife was with him. Kenny relied on her, not only for love and affection, but she was great at killing boredom.

She would play word games, tell bad jokes, or read aloud one of her many books. Mary put up with much these past two years. She came with him to every meeting. Every therapy session and stayed up with him every night when he wanted to retreat to the bottle. When he wanted to take the edge off the long day. It was taking this edge off that got him a DUI. As well as misdemeanor assault charge for yelling at a waiter when he would not bring him another drink. It was Mary that stayed with him despite his foolishness. She didn't even care about his reduced sex drive. He loved her for the time she spent with him, and he loved her for doing his best to recover. However, she didn't come with him to get his eleven-mouth chip and to tell his story in Reno. She smiled and said that she would be with him for his gold one-year chip but there were deadlines. So just this once she didn't go with him. So, Kenny found himself traveling alone to Nevada, to a city and state notorious for excess, vice, and bad behavior. He felt he was up to the task of resisting the bottle.

Kenny felt a certain amount of pride that he could drive by all the bars and Casinos in Reno and make it to his meeting. He arrived at the convention center, gave his speech, received his eleven-mouth chip, and proclaimed that "recovery is possible." He was given the customary applause, he drank coffee, and after the meeting he networked with people he had only talked with on message boards. He even cried. The whole meeting had been a cathartic release. He wished Mary was with him. But he was glad about the progress he made.

That was in the light of the waning day, and the dark of night had now settled in on the land. Now, on the drive home Kenny felt jittery and exhausted. Kenny's muscles where tense and his eyes throbbed from either strain or caffeine. His lips where dry, and he couldn't stop licking them as he tried to get moister back. The music on his phone blared a mixture of rock and jazz. His whole muscle library on shuffle, he was surprised at just how much music he had. He didn't expect he had so much hip hop. Mary's contribution he thought, as he felt the momentum of a curb on his body as he hurtled around a tight bend in the road. Kendrick Lamar *Swimming Pool* started playing, and while Kenny couldn't name the song himself, he identified with the sentiment of the lyrics.

When the music faded the island beat of Robert Holmes, *Escape* kicked in. An uncomfortable coincidence, that he got two songs about alcohol back-to-back.

Kenny dimmed his high beams every time a car showed up out of the oily pitch, something the other cars did likewise. However, the dark felt suffocating when he did this.

He forgot about piña coladas for a few minutes as he tried to pass a much slower semi in front of him. A frightful maneuver in the night as the bends and turns in California mountains were frequent and any moment another car could collide with Kenny. None ever did, but the maneuver of passing a large truck still left his heart racing. While his heart slowed down, he realized Tom *Waits, Warm beer and Cold Women* was playing. This stopped being funny, and Kenny realized he would have to have a word with Mary about the type of music they got from now on. It wasn't enough that he remembered his addiction with every waking moment, without it invading his music. He unplugged his phone from the car's radio and flipped on a local station. It was impossible for him to put in a CD at this speed, so he just had to hope that there was something besides religious radio or conservative talk shows on. There was, in the form of oldies blues.

"That last track was ever so lovely and ever so tragic, Billy holiday, with her Classic *Solitude*," Chimed in the late-night DJ. Kenny imagined a bespectacled, dread locked, stoner on the other side of the airwaves. The man's real visage was just as obscure to Kenny as any direction outside the car. Once again, he dimmed his headlights to let a passing car go by unblinded. The other driver did not do the same and for a moment Kenny was blind as the light overtook him before once again vanishing, plunging him into black ink. He cursed the driver under his breath as he regained orientation.

"You're going to love this next track, it's like glass man. Its Muddy Waters, *Sittin Here Drinking*."

"What the hell?" Kenny said an exasperated and now

irritable. He turned the radio off and just drove in silence. The silence of the radio created a stretched temporal effect where one minute felt like ten. Out in the distance Kenny could see a line of lights on the road. Like a glowing snake that closed in on him. He watched this radiant sea serpent advance, and Kenny realized that it was a line of vehicles going down a hill. A trail of smaller cars trying to pass a lumbering semi that legally had to go ten miles slower than everyone else. The trucks' high beams where on full blast, an overpowering wall of light with the truck covered in lights across all the edges of the trailer. Kenny thought of the truck drivers in Japan, who tried to get as many flashing lights on their rigs as possible each trying to out dazzle their rivals. Kenny just hoped he wasn't straying into the lane of the oncoming semi as he passed the bastion of light that would turn his little vehicle into a mass of tangled metal, crushing it as easily as if where wet cardboard. It was over in a moment, and he was once again in the dark and it seemed more oppressive than ever. He could barely see the road with his normal headlights, and he relied more and more on his high beams.

The sound of the roaring road and the ach in his shoulders felt like his only sensory input. With the inky black of the night all around him he could look at nothing but the road. He flipped the radio on and hoped that "happy hour" would stop invading his music. It was at this moment of fiddling with the radio that he took a life.

A grey bird-like blob flew out of the darkness as it dove across the road. Several thoughts invaded his mind as the blob invaded his space. His mind shouted stop! Keep driving! Death if I slam on the brakes. Then a hollow impact of the animal reverberated through the car as it hit the window. Kenny kept speeding along, not stopping as he cut through the dark. The bird must have been an owl. What other large flying thing would be swooping this late at night. With miles of darkness why did it have to fly into the road at that instant? Mabey the owl was trapped in the radiance of his car, like a fish attracted to an angler's lure in the deep sea. Every so often he tore his eyes away from the road to see if there were any cracks in his window. He couldn't tell, but he felt positive the only thing that was broken was the poor animal. Kenny felt bad, but what could he do? Hopefully it died on impact and wasn't writhing on the road in agony. Its life reduced to a twisted mess of feathers and snapped bones, eyes squinting at the abyss of the black above. Its beak sighing out weak hoots of pain.

The radio played a country song that he couldn't place. A twangy number that stretched an aching note like a bent bow. He exhaled already forgetting about the dying bird as he adjusted himself in his seat. His lower back was tense, and his shoulders burned with a tight ache.

The radio started losing reception as static crept in. The mountains must be blocking the signal, though Kenny. He hit the seek button looking for any station that was playing, but there was only static. He went through the rotation of stations twice and was about to give up when he heard a voice within the static. It was indistinct at first, an intelligible vocalization in the storm of static. Kenny still had a hundred and twenty miles to go, and he would be damned if he was listening to two hours of silence.

"Hey," the radio said before being muffled by the static. "Hey," it said again before being drowned out. Must be a local right wing nutjob with a radio license.

"Hey Kenny," said the radio, the static vanishing in an instant. For a moment Kenny was confused. His attention was mostly on the road.

"Hey Kenny, how you are doing?" Fear latched on to Kenny as if he where bitten by a shark. He was about to slow down when a car from behind him appeared from around a bend. This distracted him briefly from the voice on the radio.

"Ignore the car Ken, I'm trying to talk to you," The dark seemed to have encroached right up to Kenny's front bumper. He felt like he was driving through tar. He began to slow down.

"Don't do that Ken, the guy might not see you. You've got to maintain your speed." For a moment, Kenny felt like being obstinate. But a strange voice was calling him out over the radio, so he went back up to seventy.

"What the hell is going on?" Kenny said to himself. The speeding car roared right up to his bumper before immediately applying the breaks. The driver blared his horn before zipping around Kenny still honking as he raced through the night.

"Ignore that jerk, Ken, we got to talk, man to man," The voice reminded Kenny of a mobster. A small-time crook who wringed his hands when he was in the middle of a scam. This was too weird, he changed stations. Mabey this wasn't happening. Mabey it was an auditory hallucination, induced by the stress of driving on a country road in the middle of the night.

"That's not goanna work Ken," said the radio. Kenny slowed down around a curve. Once he finished turning, he switched the radio off. He felt he was cracking up. He wanted to be home with Mary.

"Stay with me, Ken," said the radio as it switched back on. "We got to talk; you're being difficult."

"Talk about what?" he asked, feeling both foolish and a little scared. He licked his chapped lips trying to get moisture back into them.

"You see, Kenny, I've been watching you since you left Reno. I got to say you look tense. Like a guy who has been trapped inside a coffin, and he realized he can't get out because he is being buried. You look like a guy who hears the dirt as it piles up on the lid as his world is shrunk down to a tiny box."

"What is going on, who are you, and how are you talking to me? Did you slip a microphone in my car or something? Is this some weird psycho game?"

"No game, Kenny, and there's no microphone. That would be too rational, that would make sense. We both know the world don't make sense, does it Ken? A sensible world wouldn't have an owl fly out of the dark, colliding with the only point of light in a wasteland of darkness," The car suddenly rocked as if something landed on top of it. Kenny immediately hit the brakes. All he got was soft resistance while the car kept its speed. Panic began to set in as stamped on the pedal.

"We can't stop now, Ken, you just keep driving. You've got such a long night ahead of you."

"Why are you doing this? Who are you? Why are you harassing me like this?" asked Kenny, his hands white knuckled around the steering wheel. He decided to turn off the engine to gently glide to a halt. The car remained in motion, the lights and engine remained on. Worse, he was advancing on a sharp bend. Normally he would drop speed around a turn like this, but with his current predicament he had to take a fifty-mile curve at seventy. Only he wasn't going seventy, he was speeding at seventy-five now. He didn't even have his foot on the pedal. He felt the force of the turn in his body and the weight of the car. It was a too sharp a turn and he felt he was about to lose control of the car.

"Pay attention, Ken, I Know how hard it is for a guy like you. You're the middle of the road type. You're like a rabbit, easily startled by unexpected events and loud noises," A sudden shriek of what sounded like nails tearing at the roof of his car, like a fork on a metal plate. The screeching metal clawed at his attention as he struggled to keep the car from flipping. "So, I decided to give you something."

"Oh god," Ken whispered. "Please let this be a dream. Please let this be a nightmare. Please get me home safe."

"God don't got nothing to do with this, Kenny," Said the radio "Check the glove compartment. I wonder why nobody keeps gloves in their anymore. They keep documents, don't you think that's weird, Ken? But I guess document compartment doesn't roll of the tongue."

Kenny took a deep breath. He wanted to scream. He

wanted to stop and deal with his suddenly very unbearable nervousness. Instead, he opened the glove compartment. A golden light shown from the interior and resting on the car's documents was a bottle of whisky. The bottle's label was torn off, and it was topped with a black plastic cap. The amber liquid looked like honey in the dim light.

"No, no, no, no, no," Kenny said shutting the glove compartment, "This is messed up," he held tight his eleven-month sobriety chip. "I don't want it."

"Sure you do, Ken, why else would you keep going to those meetings? If you really wanted to quit, you would have done so and stopped thinking about booze entirely. No, you constantly go to those meetings you don't want to forget. You wanted to be continually reminded about the things you can't have anymore."

"That's not true! I quit for my wife! I quit for me, and I certainly won't start because some…thing on a California backroad wants me to start again."

"Don't lie to me, Ken, lie to yourself, or to that slut Mary all you want, but don't lie to me."

"She is not a...that," Kenny rolled down the window and threw the bottle out into the inky void. The wind roared in his ear as he rolled up the window, replaced by the low hum of the road.

"Kenny, it's a sin to waste good whisky. Isn't that what you used to say all the time? It's ok, I'm not goanna let you sin tonight. I'll put that bottle back where it belongs," said the radio with a low cackle. Impossible, thought Kenny as he looked in the glove compartment again. For a moment, Kenny had to process what he was seeing. The bottle of amber whisky was there. It was the same bottle he had thrown out the window. It seemed to glow, like the breaking dawn.

"Anyway, your Mary is the biggest horndog around. She felt guilty wanting it so much these last eleven mouths. It only became worse when the booze withdraws set in and your sex drive went down the drain. She never felt guilty with Arthur."

"Her editor? No! Mary wouldn't do that! She loves me, and she would have said something!" Kenny was shouting. He was flustered. His pulse pounded in his neck and behind his eyes.

"You sure? She has been working on that deadline for a while. That's quite a bit of time with another man. Awfully convenient that you went off to Reno, wasn't it?"

"Whatever messed up game you're playing I'm not buying it," said Kenny as he slammed shut the glove compartment.

"Suit yourself, Kenny, I just wanted to give you something, you know, to take the edge off. After all, Mary's gets to have her little vice, why not have your own. What's the harm? See you around Ken," The car rocked again as if something jumped off the roof. Kenny felt a sudden drop in speed as the car was once again under his control. He signaled that he was pulling off the road, before stopping. Once again, he reached into the glove box and grabbed the whisky before getting out of the car. The air was cold, typical for norther California in the winter. Kenny didn't notice that one of his headlights was out. So, intent on getting to the side of the road. He gripped the neck of the bottle and threw it as hard as he could into the darkness of the California wild.

When he got back to his car, he noticed the bottle sitting in the driver's seat. Kenny stood on the highway looking at the dirt covered bottle, he felt like a fish who was in the glowing light of an angler's lure. The engine of the car kept running as he looked at the bottle, he shut the door of the car and began to pace. He pulled out a brand-new chap stick he bought at a gas station earlier that day. His dry lips soon felt relief as the moister was sealed in, revitalizing a small portion of his psyche.

He grabbed the bottle once again from the driver's seat, uncorked it and tried not to think about the woody aroma that seemed to cut through the night air, or the golden liquid that had a pulsing shiny glow. He turned the bottle over and poured it out onto the asphalt. To Kenny the roar of the wind was a light breeze to the sound of liquid hitting the road. He felt the warm liquid through the glass as it emptied onto Highway 395. He then dropped the bottle when he knew it was empty. He kept an eye on it as it lay on the highway like an exsanguinated corpse. Upon closing the door, he drove off back to Alturas.

He prayed that this ghastly night would soon be over, he flexed his hands on the steering wheel. He stretched the tension out of his joints. Another bend rolled up toward the car and once again he gently pressed the break to slow his speed for the turn. He met the resistance of something caught under the pedal.

Something was under the break, and Kenny had a sudden terrifying realization about what it was. He hugged the curve at an uncomfortable speed. His breathing became heavy and ragged. He kicked the bottle from underneath the break when he hit a straight road before once again slowing to a halt. He picked up the bottle and saw the golden liquid even in the dark of night. He suspected that it was the same alcohol he poured out on the road. Yet there wasn't a spec of gravel or dirt floating in the honey-colored liquid. He got out of the car again and taking the neck of the bottle, Kenny slammed the glass vessel on the asphalt. It didn't break initially, he swung it twice before the bottle shattered the smoky warm liquid once again meeting Highway 395.

He felt like he had just murdered someone. He turned to the shadows that coiled around him like a large constricting snake. He screamed into the night. It was not as loud as he thought it would be and his throat was sore from the sudden explosive voice.

"Leave me alone, I don't want to be that man anymore. I don't want to be the man the drink makes me. Whatever you are out in the dark, know that I don't want this," He said pointing at the bottle, "That stuff will ruin me. If you put in the car again it means you want to kill me. Please, I have done nothing wrong, I haven't hurt anybody. I have come close, but because of my sobriety and the people in my life I know I can change. That I have changed. I don't deserve this, I have done nothing wrong," he said breathing heavily, his voice horse. He collapsed on the road hitting the ground with his fists, feeling tears well up in his eyes. "I don't deserve this. I have done nothing wrong."

In the distance he heard the hoot of an owl. Then another one. Then the night air was filled with angry owl calls. From the darkness he heard the birds. It sounded like there were dozens of them. He stood up slowly, looking over, he saw that the bottle sat on the asphalt as pristine and unblemished as if it had just rolled out of the bottling plant.

The darkness closed in on Kenny, the light from the high beams where stifled embers in the darkness. The impulsive lizard brain took over, and Kenny rushed into the car and once again drove off at high speeds. The radio flipped on, and Kenny was barraged by the screeching of hooting owls. He drove for what felt like hours in the dark, the hooting owls sounding like a flock of admonishers. He counted the miles on the speedometer, as the onslaught of hooting on the radio grew louder. It became overwhelming for Kenny, and he found it impossible to drive. No concert had ever been this loud, no roar of jet engines, or clanking of construction equipment could meet this intense cacophony of hoots. His ears hurt as the noise assaulted him. Once again, he slowed down. He gripped his ears. He screamed but heard nothing but the hooting. His own lamentation was drowned out by the persecution of birds. He hit the steering wheel of his car. He wanted to get out, he wanted to flee on foot down the road. But something in the dark was after him. He didn't know what was out there. Even as his hearing was overwhelmed at least he had the light to see. Out there was a complete absence of light, just the darkness of the road and whatever was out there.

A gentle tap on the window cut through the cacophony, his world became silent before smooth jazz played over the radio.

"Roll down your window, sir," Kenny saw that a police officer was shining a light on him. Kenny felt terrible, he was jittery as the adrenalin coursed through him telling him to run.

The primeval instinct that was of little help dealing with a police officer. Kenny complied rolling down his window. "Are you alright sir, you seem a little agitated," said the officer.

"I'm fine," Kenny said taking a deep breath. "I'm fine. I have been driving a long way today and it's been kind of stressful."

"Turn off your radio sir," Kenny complied, the smooth jazz cut out in the middle of its soulful bars. The police officer shined his light in the car looking around the vehicle. "You been drinking tonight?" asked the officer. His light shining on the bottle had caused so much recent torment.

"No sir," said Kenny looking at the bottle trying to find an excuse as to why it was in the passenger's seat.

A Gradient into Shadows

"Can I see your license and registration sir," said the officer.

"I'm reaching for the glove compartment," he told the office imagining all the recent police shootings from the news. Kenny retrieved the documents and handed them to the police officer. Kenny saw that the name Sunderland displayed on the officer's badge. "Did you know that one of your headlights is out?" he asked, comparing Kenny's face to his driver's license.

"No sir," Kenny responded, he didn't normally say sir or ma'am, but he was trying it now. "I hit a bird earlier that must have taken it out."

The police officer said nothing as he left Kenny in the dark. Kenny watched the man returning to the spinning red and blue lights of the squad car. For several minutes Kenny was left in his car half terrified that he might get in trouble with the law, but at least he was in a scenario that was normal, not harassed by dark entities. When the police officer returned Kenny had calmed down considerable.

"Alright sir, it says that you have history of drunk driving and assault, so I am going to have to ask you again, have you been drinking tonight."

"No officer, I, actually just got my eleven-mouth chip tonight," Kenny said holding up his red chip. "I don't know why I have a bottle of alcohol in the car, maybe it was put they're at the Reno convention. A bad joke, I suppose."

"A bad joke. Where are you headed tonight."

"Alturas sir, I live down there."

"Well, you have had no incidents in the last eleven mouths so I'm going to let you off with a verbal warning, I advise you to check into a hotel in the next town. Get some sleep and get your headlights fixed in the morning. As for that bottle of whisky, that cap stays on."

"Yes, sir," Kenny said, as the officer handed back his documents. "Officer, could you dispose of this. I don't think I can have it in the car, and I can't seem to get rid of it," he said handing the bottle too officer Sunderland. The man was suspicious but took the bottle.

"I'm afraid I can't do that Kenny," said officer Sunderland before the radio flipped on again, and the same voice from the dark, spoke in unison with officer Sunderland. "It's a sin to waste good whisky."

Kenny then awoke suddenly while still driving down the highway. He had nodded off, and a curb was fast approaching. He slammed on the breaks turning hard to try and not hit the edge of the road. The vehicle squealed as he lost control. He crashed into the guard rail and flew off the road into the ditch at over seventy miles an hour. The car flipped and crumpled. Kenny died before the car had a chance to settle at the bottom of a deep ravine.

In the morning after a motorist had called in the crash and after the police and corners had done their job. Officer Sunderland and his colleague Officer White were talking on the side of the road, each holding a Styrofoam cup of coffee.

"That's when I told him I would be glad to pour out the bottle, but who knows if he drank anything before, but I was willing to give him the benefit of the doubt," said Sunderland.

"That's unfortunate."

"He seemed pretty shaken up about something. I guess we will find out in a couple days on that tox screen if he was drinking or not. Who knows he might have just fallen asleep at the wheel. At least he didn't take anyone with him."

"Small mercies, I guess," said Officer White.

"Mabey, right now the only thing for certain is that he crashed and only he and the road knows why?"

Under the officers' feet, beneath the road, hidden from the sunlight, something snickered as it waited for night fall once again.

A Gradient into Shadows

Down the Mine Shaft

Darkness clawed at the edge of the elevator as Daddy, and I descended the mine shaft. The elevator rattled as it slowly lowered us into the earth. I could feel my breath become heavy, and my stomach tightened. I had never been that deep in the mines before. Not ever. I didn't want to be there. I wanted to be in bed. It was a school night, and I had a test the next day. But when Daddy says, "Wake up we're going for a ride," you don't argue. You don't ever argue. If you do, you get bruises.

"Here we are, rock bottom," he said, opening the gate. "Let's go. We have two miles of mountain to travel, and we don't have all night."

I followed him to a minecart that was barely three feet high. I hopped into the side seat and adjusted the straps on my helmet so it wouldn't dig into my neck.

"Daniel! Stop fucking with your helmet. If something goes wrong down here that might be the only thing that can save your life."

"OK, Daddy."

As the engine started, Daddy began to drive down the square hallway of the mine. As we moved down the corridor the roof began to shrink down until there was only a few inches between us and the ceiling. I could have reached up and dragged my hand across all that coal, but I didn't want to upset Daddy. Instead, I counted the bolts in the ceiling as they passed. I tried not to think about the knife at Daddy's hip. He never brought it with him unless he was going to skin something. Like one of the small rabbits from our hutches. As far as I knew there were no rabbits down here. Just Daddy and me. Now that I thought about it the mines would be a great place to hide a small body like my own.

"Daddy, what are those bolts for?" I asked.

"They keep the ceiling from collapsing on us."

"How's that?"

"Just know that if they weren't there, the mountain would come crashing down on us."

It was then that I felt the shrinking tunnel, the weight of billions of tons of rock and coal above me. I tightened my jacket to keep out the cold. Daddy never mentioned how cold it was down there. As cold as winter, but much darker. Our only illumination was the small cart's front lights and our headlamps that pierced the swirling black dust. We stopped at the end of the corridor and Daddy crawled out on his knees.

"Come on, son, move your ass," he said, as I crawled out of the cart. I hadn't hit my growth spurt just yet, that would be a few years off, but I was still too tall for the cramped quarters of the mine. I crawled on my knees over jagged lumps of coal that left bruises. My lamp lit up Daddy's blue denim jacket as he led me to the very back of the shaft. It was there that we found a tiny hollow that was as wide and tall as a crouched man.

"Here it is," he said, pointing to the small alcove, "Go

on, son, take a look."

Inside the alcove was a bronze statue of a nude woman covered with dark brown paint that rolled off her head and down her metal body. Piles of cigarettes and fruit were placed around it, as well as a dead rabbit.

"What is it?" I asked.

"A shrine," he said, leaning against the uncut wall of coal. "Like the shrines you will find in some of the mines in South America. The ones that give offering to El Tio, lord of the underworld. The miners there believe that once you're below the earth, you're no longer in God's realm but El Tio's. So, they give offerings to him for their safety. Offerings of cigarettes, food, and the occasional sacrifice of a llama. This is not a shrine to El Tio, this is a shrine to Ellishtaara."

I looked back at the statue, something in me jolted with excitement and confusion.

"Daddy I..."

"Spit it out, boy, down here we can speak freely. There can only be truth down under the mountain, down in this underworld away from God's eyes," he said. I realized he looked calmer. When he was at home, he had this tense look about him, like a mousetrap always ready to snap.

"It's just that Pastor Ryan told us about the Ten Commandments given to us by Moses," I said, scooting away from the idol to look at my father.

"Did he now?"

"Are you worshiping this statue?"

"Yes," he sighed with relief.

"But that breaks the first two commandments: *Thou shalt have no other God before me, Thou shalt not bow to any false idols or graven images.*"

"That it does."

"But why? God has given us so much. Why would you turn your back on him? Don't you love God?" I asked. My daddy's eyes lit up as he leaned in real close to me.

"Do I love God? Daniel, remember what God did to us! He tried to drown us when we were not properly obedient to his will. He cast us out of Eden! He cursed us with fractured languages for making a tower too tall! I do not love God, Daniel, I hate God! I hate how he erodes our community and takes away the jobs of hard-working men. I hate how he forgives us for being the flawed creatures that he made."

As he spoke, he picked up a chunk of coal and threw it against the wall, sending a clacking reverberation through the mountain.

"I hate how I'm trying to make an honest living digging up coal as the rest of the world goes to shit. I hate how our town gets poorer as the bastards in Washington and Wall Street get richer. We have played by God's rules and where has it gotten us? A rusting shit-hole town on the brink of collapse. That's gonna change."

Normally, I'd have fled to my room, held my little sister, Emma, tight to keep her from crying. To keep me from crying. But there was nowhere I could go in this mine. I was trapped in this suffocating darkness.

"So how is this statue supposed to help?" I said, trying to ground him back in the world. Back from his supposed enemies that persecuted him.

"This is not just a statue, Daniel. This is a goddess. A physical, real goddess. Ellishtaara was found in a construction site during the reign of Fayṣal ibn Ghāzī ibn Fayṣal Āl Hāshim, the last king of Iraq. She was placed in a museum where her power was stripped from her. She was not the object of worship. She had become a sterile exhibit.

"She even had a little card that explained how she was the local goddess of a tiny village off the Euphrates, and that the city of Babylon had kidnapped her to enforce tithes and subservience. The officials of Babylon even gave the village a receipt made of clay. When Babylon was burned to the ground, she was lost to history until she was found, three thousand years later."

"Why is she here? In Virginia?" I asked, looking at the stained statue and the offerings around it.

"That's where I come into the story," he said, showing me his Gulf War veteran's patch. "There was lots of looting in that war. Could be a simple as money, or medical supplies, but also cultural artifacts; small ancient things that can be hidden in a suitcase that can be sold for hundreds or thousands of dollars. Some museum curator had Ellishtaara packed away in bubble wrap with all the research notes and a certificate of authenticity. I confiscated his suitcase and had him arrested. Only I kept Ellishtaara. I wanted a souvenir and what I got instead was our salvation."

"How is that?" I asked, adjusting my jacket against the cold. Much of what Daddy said to me was going over my head but I figured if I steered him to the point, we could leave that terrible mine.

"Use your head, Daniel. God decided to let our town rot. Fewer miners making an honest living out here. We were wasting away. Then I started worshiping Ellishtaara, real quiet at first. I began to give her scraps of my lunch, then I began to win scratch lottery tickets. When I gave her other things like incense and a shrine, I was offered a few stock shares in the company. It didn't take long for the other fellas to get in on the action. Accidents were down, and the mine was no longer in the red. I can tell they are not as devout as me. To them, she is just a good luck charm. But I began to ask the question, what would a larger sacrifice achieve? A proper sacrifice of blood."

I turned to the idol, and I finally realized what the brown substance was. Realized where he took those baby rabbits from our hutches. The ones he claimed were too thin to survive winter. It was why he always bought two ducks for Christmas, one living, one dead. I then became aware of the knife at his hip and the realization that he did not particularly like me.

"Gods are such hungry things," he said to no one. He wasn't talking to me. He just needed a way of voicing all these weird notions he had. "Some can live on nothing but incense, for other gods only the taste of human flesh could satiate their hunger. The Christian God is no better; he survives on our ritual, through the miracle of transubstantiation we eat him, and he is fed by our devotion. That's the key, isn't it? He was just a tiny god, like Ellishtaara. But through the sacrifice of a being without sin, his body made flesh in the form of his son; he became bigger than the desert he came from."

"You haven't done that, have you? Sacrificed any people?" I asked, scared to know the answer.

"Daniel don't be stupid," he said, turning to the shrine. I gave a small sigh of relief, thankful that my father was not a murderer. "I just haven't found anyone without sin."

"Oh," was all I could say. The silence from that response was devoured by the mountain. "Uh...um."

"Spit it out, Daniel."

"Why do we keep going to church? Isn't that a problem for Ellishtaara?" I said, pointing at the idol.

"It is, but what we are doing down here must be kept secret from God. That's why our worship of Ellishtaara must be done under the mountain, hidden from his sight. Down here he can see nothing. Up there we appear as his devout servants, enduring his attention as Job had done before us."

"Does Mom know about Ellishtaara?"

"No, and you must never tell her. She is a good Christian woman, a good meek lamb who doesn't know what's good for her. She is easily spooked, that's why I keep a firm hand with her," he said, flexing his rough hands into fists.

"Why are you showing me this?" I asked.

"Because you will be continuing my work. I am making the foundations for our new church. You must be the one to lead it. You will be its inheritor as we usher in Ellishtaara's magnificence into our world. Do you understand, Daniel?" He then grabbed me by the shoulders and squeezed me so tight it hurt. "Do you understand? Tell me you understand." He was shouting, his pleas echoing throughout the mine shaft.

"Yes!" I lied. "I understand!"

"Don't lie to me, boy, I know you are prone to white lies!"

"I'm not lying, Daddy!" I shouted.

"Then prove it," he said, drawing his knife and handing it to me. I held the knife by the thick wooden handle. It was heavier than I expected.

"How do I prove it with this?"

He held up his hand to reveal the giant scar that connected the webbing between his thumb and index finger.

"But that will hurt," I said.

"Of course, if it didn't, then it wouldn't mean a damn thing, now would it."

"Do I have to?"

"Daniel," growled my father through gritted teeth. "Don't be a fucking pansy-ass; be a fucking man. Just put the edge of the blade against your palm, grip the blade tight, and pull."

I did as I was told and squeezed the knife. But not hard enough to cut. I was too afraid of the knife's edge. I was holding back tears as that would only make things worse.

"What's the holdup? Make the cut," he said. When I didn't, he grabbed my fist that held the knife and began to squeeze. The knife's edge bit into my skin, and then into the meat of my hand.

"Daddy, it hurts!" I shouted. He only squeezed harder.

"You have to pull the knife out, son. It doesn't mean anything if I do it for you."

"It hurts, it hurts, you're hurting me!"

"If you don't pull it out soon, you're going to have permanent nerve damage. Do you want that? Do you want to lose the use of your hand?"

I gripped the handle of the knife and began to pull. The stinging slice in my hand became worse with each inch. After an agonizing few seconds, the blade was free. I dropped the knife, and it clattered onto the ground. I didn't have time to nurse the wound as Daddy took my hand and placed it on the idol. My blood leaked down over the statue and onto the coal slap that was her altar. The light from my helmet illuminated the small space, my blood standing out against the bronze.

As harrowing as that night was, I remember a feeling of tranquility fell over me such as I had never known. A feeling of peace, safety, and warmth that was absent in my home. That feeling vanished when my hand was pulled away from the idol and soaked down with rubbing alcohol. I hissed in pain as the clear liquid washed away blood, exposing the sliced meat of my hand. He pulled out a fishhook and stitches and began to reknit my bleeding hand.

"I should be making you do this," he said, sliding the hook through my ragged skin. "You did good though. I'm proud of you, son. You dragged your feet getting here, but I can't say when I did it, it was any easier." I winced each time the needle pierced my skin, but soon there was a row of stitches wrapped up with gauze.

"Now if your mother, a teacher, your sister, or whoever asks how you cut your hand you just say you cut it on some razor wire. Got it?"

"Yes, Daddy."

"Good. Now let's gets some ice cream," he said, leading me into the cart. As Daddy turned the cart around, I watched the alcove and the small bronze idol inside. With a turn of my head, it was plunged back into the darkness.

Many Years Later

"You need to come home. It's your father, I think he has finally lost his mind," she said over the phone.

"Mama, I can't drop everything each time Roger has an episode."

"This is different. He took your niece, Emma is distraught."

"What do you mean took her? How did this happen?"

"He was released from the hospital about two weeks ago, cutbacks or something. He broke the restraining order and snuck into your sister's house. He stabbed your brother-in-law."

"What! Is Jeremy, OK? Please don't tell me he is…"

"He's fine. In the hospital, nothing important was hit. Nobody knows where your father is, Daniel. There is an Amber alert out, but you need to come home. You understood him better than anyone."

She was right, only somewhat. I understood him enough that when I turned eighteen, I walked out our front door and never looked back. I made my life away from his delusions. Now I was returning to that old life on a plane back to Virginia.

I found my mother in the family house. The house she kept in the divorce. Emma was there but unconscious from a tranquilizer. I hugged Mom, before taking a serving of casserole given to the family by the neighbors.

"The police still haven't found him," Mama said lighting her cigarette. "They have been looking everywhere. He hasn't called you, has he?"

"No, Mama, the last time I talked to Roger was on Father's Day two years ago. He called me a pansy sellout before throwing a remote control at me. The nurses say that it was because of the medicine he was taking but we both know that's not true. He is just rotten like that."

"He wasn't always so mean," she said with a puff of smoke.

"Yes, he was. He was always rattlesnake mean. How's Emma doing?"

"Oh, she is a wreck. After her last miscarriage, she had just about given up on children. But with our little miracle Rose she brightened up, from storm clouds to sunshine. That was until your daddy did what he did. Poor girl. Barely had the child a month before that man did his foolishness. I have prayed all day to the Lord Jesus Christ for her safety. Poor Emma has had the worst luck; it seems this entire town's luck dried up the day you left."

"That's not my fault."

"No, I don't think it is," she said through a cloud of acrid smoke. "You just left the casino before the house turned against us. I can't blame you for that. You have been good to us. Those checks from your first book kept this family floating. But with the mine closing, there wasn't any work for good honest folks. Turns out selling crystal is a hell of a lot easier than an honest day's work."

"Are things that bad here?"

"Things aren't great. But we make do," she said, readying another cigarette. "Can I ask you something?"

"Of course," I said, taking my plate to the sink and washing it.

"What finally convinced you to get out? What was it that allowed you to break free from your Daddy's grasp while the rest of us remained clenched in his fist?" she asked. I looked down at the white scar on my palm as the water from the tap poured into the sink. I clenched my fist, thinking about the night in the mine so long ago.

"Remember when I cut myself with that razor wire that one night?"

"Yeah?"

"That was Roger's doing. I wasn't near any barbed wire that night."

"Oh, dear Lord. I'm sorry that happened, Daniel."

"Want to know what the worst part was?" I said, shutting off the water and turning to her.

"What's that?"

"We didn't get any ice cream afterward," I said with a smile. A moment later Mama snorted with laughter before tapping the ash from her cigarette into the overflowing ashtray.

"Oh Lord, I'm so sorry for laughing, darling, but that is just like him. He does something cruel and promises to make it better. Something he never delivers."

I chuckled to myself before returning to the window. It was night. The flight here was one of the darkest I had seen in a long time. Looking out at that dark I thought of Daddy and his strange ideas, and how I got that scar.

"I think I know where Daddy is," I said not looking back at Mama.

"Don't keep me waiting, I'll let Sheriff Parker know immediately."

"Not yet, I might be able to get him to give himself up. I'll go see, then we can have Sheriff Parker check it out in the morning. If I come back before then we won't have wasted the sheriff's time. If I don't come back, you know what to do."

"Are you sure that's a good idea?" asked Mama.

"Not really, but I know Roger. I might be able to convince him to return little Rose. Remember, I was the one that got him to volunteer to get committed. We have this...bond... it's hard to explain. But I believe I can get Rose back safely. With the way Roger is, I don't think the sheriff should be our first option."

"Alright darling, I'll give you till morning. But you have to tell me where he might be."

"I think he's in the old coal mines."

"Oh, honey, you can't go in there. There is a reason those mines went belly up. It just wasn't safe there anymore. Mine corridors were collapsing. I don't even think Roger is crazy enough to hide in there."

"Those mines were very important to Roger. They were more than just a livelihood. It was where he felt safe. A place where he felt he couldn't be scrutinized."

"Alright, Daniel. If Emma wakes up, I'll tell her you stopped by. But if you don't show up by tomorrow morning, I'm sending in the cavalry."

I took my rental car up the winding path of the mountain. There were no lights on that road, only the occasional reflective signs that glowed bright yellow with my headlights. Signs that said, *turn back, road closed, danger, abandoned mine ahead.* I knew these things wouldn't dissuade Daddy. He always mocked signs like that.

"If they can't tell it's dangerous, then they should get what's coming to them," he said to me once while rounding a cliff, pointing out the "falling rocks" sign.

The mine was fenced off, with a large gate with a chain on the main road. I left the car and took the flashlight that I had pulled out of Mama's kitchen drawer. It was hefty enough to use as a club. I walked over to the fence to find that the chain only appeared to be locked. The padlock was broken, allowing me to pull the chain off. There were several dilapidated buildings outside the mine's entrance. There was a truck outside the workers' locker rooms. I looked inside the truck, and I found a splatter of dried blood on the driver's seat as well as Rose's car seat. The keys rested in the cup holder along with a cut patient wrist band.

I checked the worker prep area and saw that the dust

had been disturbed. A few lockers had been opened, and I could see the hard hats and coveralls inside. I doubted the headlamps worked, but if I was going down into that mountain, I needed a hard hat. I took one and made my way to the mine's entrance. The old elevator was generator-fed. All you needed to do was put some gas in it for it to work. It was working now, even if the fluorescent lights of the shaft weren't. As I rode down, the shaft was filled with the same clattering I had heard as a child. I had the same sinking lurch in my stomach. Only now, the darkness wasn't held off by the elevator's florescent lights; now it was in the cage with me, cut away only with each swing of my flashlight before filling the void of lights absence with the dark water of shadow.

  At the bottom of the shaft, I found a cart and gas can, Daddy probably took a cart and left the can behind. I checked the tank of the remaining cart, filled it up, and started the long drive down the corridor. It wasn't long before I found the small alcove that once held Daddy's idol, but the corridor had been expanded, leaving an empty divot. I kept driving until the ceiling began to vault up. A soft glow of light began to take shape in the distance. It grew as I drove over the coal until I found a large, vaulted chamber with Daddy standing on a raised mound of coal.

"The apostate returns," boomed my father in his loose-fitting clothing. "What do you think of my cathedral? It was all I could make before the mine shut down after you left us taking our goddess' blessing with you."

"Roger, you're having an episode. There is no goddess Ellishtaara," I said, pointing my flashlight at him as I got out of the cart.

"Why she should continue giving her blessing to you is beyond me, but you can't deny it! Your six-figure book deals, your big house, beautiful wife, book tours, all of Ellishtaara's blessings come to you while I toil silently in her name!"

"Roger! Stop fucking around! Where is Rose!"

"I still your father, you shit. Goddess' blessing or not, you show some respect," he said stepping down from the coal.

"Roger. Where is Rose?"

"She is over on the other side of the coal. I wouldn't look. She is not exactly in one piece."

I ran over to the other side of the coal pile, and I recoiled in horror at the sight and turned away. My poor niece was mashed to a pulped with a large chunk of coal. I never thought Daddy would ever go this far, but the proof bled into the pile of coal.

"How could you?" I sputtered.

"I needed a sacrifice that was without sin, Daniel, like Jesus on the cross. Now Ellishtaara will have over two thousand years of worship, no longer will we bend the knee to an uncaring God. Now we will have the bounties of the world."

I charged him, using the flashlight like a club.

"Like Longinus stabbing Jesus, my act of cruelty will be the spark to a new era. That's not something a pansy-ass like you could have ever done!" he shouted.

I rained blows on his arms as he shielded his head. His body was so frail, it was hard to imagine that this skinny man had such power over my family.

The rustling of coal stopped my assault. We both turned to see the pile of coal shift and tumble as a long dusky hand erupted from the pile. A woman more beautiful and terrible than I have ever seen climbed out of the pile of black rocks. Blood and black dust clung to her nude body as she arose. With each step, she made flowers that bloomed and died in a moment, and the smell of the roaring sea hit us.

"Ellishtaara!" howled my father, knocking me aside. I was in too much shock to do anything as my father knelt before the goddess made flesh.

"I am your faithful servant, my goddess," he said, clenching his hands in prayer. The goddess looked him over as a child looked over an ant crawling on her hand. With the tip of her finger, she raised him by his chin and then tossed Daddy aside as if he were tissue paper. Her eyes turned to me.

"Him! You're going to choose that pansy-ass over the one who brought you here," said Daddy as he marched over to Ellishtaara, grabbing her by the arm like he had my mother so many times. "I demand you give me my reward for my service," he shouted.

The goddess placed her hand on his wrist and squeezed, Daddy began to scream as her grip crushed his wrist, filling the chamber with the sound of snapping bones. When he let go,

Ellishtaara pushed her hand through his rib cage as if it were nothing but water. Daddy's screaming turned into a gasping gurgle as he was thrown aside. In her hands was Daddy's heart. I watched as she crushed the organ above her head, allowing the blood to run down her face.

When she was done, she threw the heart aside like a piece of crushed fruit.

I never wanted this, I thought, getting to my knees. I didn't want any of this. She saw my thoughts as one sees a bird through a pane of glass.

"Few chosen by a god desire it, Daniel," she said in a voice that sent shockwaves of coal dust away from her.

This can't be real, I thought. This must be a delusion, the shock of my murdered niece mixed with hereditary mental illness.

"I am no phantom of a fractured mind, Daniel. I am divine power given flesh. I am!"

"But how?" I said, sinking my head to the black coal of the earth.

"Your place is not to understand. Yours is to carry my

name to the world, tell them of my holy mountain, tell them of my glory and beneficence, and they will name you, my prophet. Now rise!"

I had no choice. I rose before Ellishtaara. I dared not look upon her for hers was a beauty of a terrible hurricane. Her hands took my head and gently turned it to meet her eyes.

"With this task, I have placed upon you, you must not be distracted by other sights. You will be the only one who will truly know my image, you must hold it in your heart."

She then gouged out my eyes, leaving me blind. She was the last thing I ever saw, and while all the rest of my memories of sight have become hazy, my memory of the goddess stays etched forever in my mind in all her terrible glory. Glory to Ellishtaara. Glory to the true Goddess of the world.

Author Bio

Stuart Mascair is a self-published author, and proud member of the Cherokee Nation. He lives in Albuquerque, New Mexico where he enjoys hiking local trails. Stuart graduated from Evergreen State College with a Bachelor of Arts in political science with an emphasis on literature. In 2021, he received his Master of Fine Arts in creative writing from the Institute of American Indian Arts in Santa Fe.

When not writing, Stuart can be found jamming out to some tunes, painting little army men, trying out a new recipe, or looking for a new digital artist to inspire him.

Enjoyed A Gradient into Shadows? Check out Stuart's Novel, <u>Witch of the Winter Moon</u>. A story about, Nadia, a young Ukrainian witch discovering her place in the world during the horrors of the WW2. Nadia calls upon all her wits, knowledge, and guile to evade a dangerous Nazi witch hunter. All the while trying to discover the whereabouts of a mysterious coven. Accompanied by the tom cat Dasha, Nadia must uncover magical secretes, deal with powerful spirits, and survive horrifying battlefields, in a story of magic, adventure, and war.

You can order Witch of the Winter Moon at Barnes & Noble, Amazon, and any book store that works with EngramSpark.

Milton Keynes UK
Ingram Content Group UK Ltd.
UKHW030749221024
449869UK00004B/232